THE HOUSEMAID IS THE ENEMY

A HEART-STOPPING PSYCHOLOGICAL THRILLER FILLED WITH
UNEXPECTED TURNS THAT WILL LEAVE YOU REELING.

VICTORIA LANNE

Peartree

DEDICATION

To my family

CONTENTS

PROLOGUE

The Seeds of Vengeance

Summer, 20 years ago

The air thrummed with the low hum of cicadas and the distant splash of the fountain. The Bennett estate, a sprawling masterpiece of modern architecture, shimmered under the summer sun. It wasn't just a house; it was a statement. A monument to Robert Bennett's relentless ambition and burgeoning success. Polished chrome gleamed, reflecting the manicured lawns and sculpted hedges. Every window, a dark eye, seemed to watch as guests in elegant attire mingled on the terrace, their laughter a brittle counterpoint to the tension simmering beneath the surface.

He moved through the crowd with a predator's grace, his smile a practiced weapon. Robert Bennett, the golden boy of the business world. "The man with the Midas touch," they called him, and tonight, he was Midas himself, radiating an aura of power and invincibility. His eyes, the color of a stormy sea, scanned the room, lingering on a woman standing apart from the throng.

Isabella.

She was a quiet force, the steady hand behind Robert's meteoric rise. Her intelligence was a razor-sharp blade, cutting through the bullshit and getting to the heart of any problem. Tonight, she wore a simple black dress that clung to her curves, a stark contrast to the flamboyant gowns of the other women. Her dark hair was pulled back in a sleek ponytail, accentuating her high cheekbones and the knowing glint in her eyes.

"You're staring, Robert," a voice purred in his ear. Katherine, his fiancée, a vision of blonde perfection, slipped her arm through his. "Is there something more interesting than your engagement party?"

Robert turned to her, his smile widening. "Nothing could be more interesting than you, my dear," he murmured, his eyes never leaving Isabella.

The tension between them was a palpable thing, a silent conversation conducted in stolen glances and subtle gestures. A touch of hands on a shared document, a lingering look across a crowded conference room. It was a dangerous game they played, a high-stakes gamble with their careers and their hearts on the line.

Isabella met Robert's gaze across the room, a flicker of defiance in her eyes. She raised her glass in a silent toast, her lips curving into a smile that didn't quite reach her eyes. It was a smile that said, "I see you, Robert Bennett. I know your secrets, and I'm not afraid."

The party swirled around them, a kaleidoscope of colors and conversations. But at that moment, it was just the two of them, locked in a silent battle of wills. The unspoken words hung heavy in the air, a promise and a threat.

The summer night throbbed with the promise of something more. The hum of the air conditioner was the only sound in the otherwise silent room, a stark contrast to the turmoil brewing beneath the surface.

Robert stepped towards Isabella, his eyes burning with a hunger that had nothing to do with ambition. He reached out, his fingers tracing the line of her jaw, the curve of her neck. His touch was electric, sending shivers down her spine.

"This is madness," Isabella whispered, her voice barely a breath. But her body betrayed her words, leaning into his touch, craving the warmth of his skin against hers.

Robert's lips curved into a smile, a dangerous glint in his eyes. "Madness," he agreed, his voice a low rumble. "But oh, what glorious madness."

And then he was kissing her, his lips claiming hers with a fierce possessiveness. It was a kiss that spoke of stolen moments and hidden desires, of a love that dared not speak its name. Isabella melted into him, her arms winding around his neck, her fingers tangling in his hair.

They clung to each other as if they were drowning, their bodies a map of unspoken longing. Robert's hands roamed over her back, his touch leaving a trail of fire in its wake. Isabella gasped, her fingers digging into his shoulders as he deepened the kiss.

It was a dangerous dance they danced, a tightrope walk between passion and ruin. They both knew the risks and the potential fallout if their affair was discovered. But in that moment, none of it mattered. All that mattered was the feel of each other's bodies, the taste of each other's lips, the unspoken promise of something more.

They broke apart, their chests heaving, their eyes locked in a silent conversation. Robert reached out, his thumb brushing a stray tear from Isabella's cheek.

"We can't do this," she whispered, her voice thick with emotion. "It's wrong. It's dangerous."

Robert cupped her face in his hands, his eyes searching hers. "I know," he said, his voice barely a whisper. "But God, Isabella, I can't stay away from you."

His words were a confession, a plea, a promise. Isabella looked into his eyes, and at that moment, she knew she was lost.

They fell into each other's arms again, their bodies entwined, their souls bared. In the quiet of the empty office, they found solace and surrender, their love a fragile flame flickering in the darkness.

The risk was real, the danger palpable. But in that moment, all that mattered was the intoxicating thrill of the forbidden, the intoxicating power of their love.

The ornate dining room of the De Luca residence was a far cry from the sleek lines of Robert's office. It was a place of heavy mahogany furniture, antique oil paintings, and an atmosphere thick with tradition and unspoken expectations.

Isabella sat across from her parents, her hands clasped tightly in her lap. The tension in the room was as tangible as the silver cutlery gleaming under the chandelier. Her father, a stern-faced man with a voice like gravel, cleared his throat.

"Isabella," he began, his tone measured but firm, "we need to talk about this… infatuation of yours."

Her mother, a picture of elegant disapproval, nodded in agreement. "Darling, Robert Bennett is not the kind of man we envisioned for you. He's… ambitious, yes, but there's a ruthlessness about him, a disregard for tradition and decorum. He's not our kind."

Isabella's jaw tightened. "He's a brilliant businessman, Papa.

He's building an empire."

Her father scoffed. "An empire built on sand. He cuts corners, He's not stable, Isabella. Not the kind of man who can keep a family."

"That's not true papa," Isabella retorted, her voice rising.

Her mother reached across the table, her hand a gentle but firm grip on Isabella's wrist. "My dear, we only want what's best for you. A secure future, a respectable husband, a family of your own."

"Robert and I..." Isabella began, but her mother cut her off.

"Robert Bennett will never marry you, Isabella. He's not interested in settling down. He's interested in climbing the ladder, in making his mark on the world. And you, my dear, will be left behind, with nothing but a broken heart and a tarnished reputation."

Isabella's eyes filled with tears. "You don't understand," she whispered. "I love him."

Her father's face hardened. "Love is a luxury, Isabella. A luxury we cannot afford. You will end this foolish affair, or you will no longer be welcome in this house."

The ultimatum hung heavy in the air, the unspoken threat clear. Isabella looked from her father to her mother, their faces a mask of disappointment and disapproval. Her heart ached with the knowledge that she was about to make a choice that would change her life forever. But at that moment, she knew she couldn't give up Robert, not without a fight.

The dinner ended in silence, the unspoken words echoing in the heavy air. Isabella left the room with her head held high, her resolve strengthened by the opposition she faced. She knew the road ahead would be difficult, but she was determined to fight for her love, even if it meant sacrificing everything she had ever known.

The moon cast long shadows across Isabella's bedroom, painting the walls with an ethereal glow. She sat on the edge of her bed, her fingers tracing the intricate pattern of the lace bedspread. Her mind was a battlefield, her heart a hostage in a tug-of-war between love and duty.

On one side, there was her family, her blood, her roots. The De Lucas were a proud lineage, their name synonymous with tradition and honor. They had instilled in her a deep sense of responsibility, a belief that family always came first. To defy them, to choose a man they deemed unworthy, would be a betrayal of everything she had been taught.

But on the other side, there was Robert. He was a fire that burned bright, a force of nature that swept her off her feet. He was ambition personified, a man who dared to dream big and had the audacity to chase those dreams with relentless passion. He saw in her a partner, a confidante, a woman who could match his intellect and his drive. He made her feel alive, as if anything was possible as long as they were together.

Her heart ached with the thought of losing him, of never feeling the warmth of his touch, the thrill of his kiss, the comfort of his presence. He was her escape from the stifling confines of her family's expectations, her chance to forge her own path, to live a life on her own terms.

Isabella closed her eyes, her breath hitching in her throat. Images of her future flashed before her eyes:

A life with Robert, filled with passion, adventure, and the thrill of building something together. A life where she was valued for her mind, her spirit, her ambition. A life where she was truly loved.

A life without Robert, filled with empty social gatherings, loveless marriage prospects, and the stifling weight of her family's disapproval. A life where she was a pawn in their game of appearances, a dutiful daughter, a respectable wife, but never truly herself.

The choice was agonizing, the stakes impossibly high. But as the night wore on, as the moon climbed higher in the sky, a clarity settled over Isabella. She knew what she had to do.

Love, she realized, was not a luxury, but a necessity. It was the fuel that ignited the soul, the spark that gave life meaning. To deny it, to sacrifice it on the altar of duty, would be to betray her own heart.

With a newfound resolve, Isabella made her decision. She would choose love, even if it meant losing her family. She would embrace the uncertainty of the future, the risks, the challenges. She would stand by Robert's side, her love a shield against the storms that were sure to come.

It was a gamble, a leap of faith into the unknown. But as Isabella opened her eyes to the dawn, a sense of peace settled over her. She had chosen love, and in that choice, she had found her freedom.

The opulent boardroom, usually a stage for Robert's triumphs, now felt like a suffocating prison. The air hung heavy with unspoken tension, the mahogany table a chasm between them. Isabella sat across from him, her hands trembling slightly as she held a small, white envelope.

"Robert," she began, her voice barely a whisper, "I need to tell you something."

He leaned back in his leather chair, his fingers steepled under his chin. "What is it, Isabella?" he asked, his voice smooth, his eyes unreadable.

She took a deep breath, her heart pounding in her chest. "I'm pregnant."

The words hung in the air, a silent bomb waiting to detonate. Robert's expression remained unchanged, but a muscle twitched in his jaw.

"Pregnant?" he repeated, his voice devoid of emotion.

Isabella nodded, her eyes pleading for understanding, for compassion. But she found none.

"This is... unexpected," Robert said, his tone measured, his words carefully chosen. "We were careful, weren't we?"

A wave of nausea washed over Isabella. "Yes, but sometimes... accidents happen."

Robert rose from his chair, pacing the length of the boardroom, his hands clasped behind his back. "Accidents," he mused, as if weighing the word on his tongue. "Unfortunate accidents."

He stopped in front of the window, staring out at the city skyline, his back to Isabella. "This complicates things," he said, his voice barely audible.

"Complicates things?" Isabella echoed, her voice laced with hurt and disbelief. "You're talking about our child, Robert. Our child!"

He turned to face her, his eyes cold, his expression impassive. "Our child," he repeated, as if tasting the words for the first time. "A child that will jeopardize everything I've worked for. My career, my reputation, my future."

Isabella's heart sank. This wasn't the Robert she loved, the man who whispered sweet nothings in her ear, the man who made her feel cherished and desired. This was a stranger, a cold, calculating businessman who saw their child as nothing more than an obstacle to his ambition.

"I won't let you ruin my life, Isabella," Robert said, his voice now edged with steel. "I won't let this child ruin everything I've built."

Isabella's vision blurred with tears. "What are you saying?" she whispered.

Robert's gaze was unwavering, his words cutting through her like a knife. "I'm saying that this child cannot be born. I'm saying that you need to take care of this."

His words echoed in the silence of the boardroom, each syllable a blow to Isabella's heart. She stared at him in disbelief, her world crumbling around her. The love she once felt for him curdled into something cold and bitter, a seed of resentment planted deep within her soul.

The opulent façade of Robert's office felt like a cruel mockery now. The tastefully chosen art, the expensive furnishings, the sweeping view of the city – they were all symbols of a life Isabella was about to lose.

"Robert, you can't mean what you're saying," she pleaded, her voice trembling. "This is our child. A part of you, a part of me."

Robert's jaw tightened. He turned away from her, his gaze fixed on the cityscape below. "Isabella," he began, his voice low and controlled, "we both knew the risks. We both knew this was a possibility."

"But we didn't plan for it," she countered, her voice rising. "We didn't want it. But it's here now, and we have a responsibility."

He whirled around, his eyes flashing with anger. "Responsibility?" he spat the word out like a curse. "You talk to me of responsibility? This child is a liability, Isabella. A liability I cannot afford."

"A liability?" she repeated, her voice choked with emotion. "Is that how you see our child? A liability?"

"Don't be dramatic," Robert snapped, his patience wearing

thin. "This is business, Isabella. And in business, you have to make tough decisions. Sometimes, you have to sacrifice the personal for the professional."

Isabella's heart sank as she realized the depth of his callousness. The man she loved, the man she had given her heart and her loyalty to, was a stranger. A cold, ruthless stranger who valued his ambition above all else.

"So that's it then?" she asked, her voice hollow. "You're willing to sacrifice our child, our love, for your career?"

"Don't put it like that," Robert said, his tone softening slightly. "It's not about sacrificing love. It's about being practical, about making the right choice for both of our futures."

"Our futures?" Isabella scoffed. "What future is there for us if we're willing to abandon our own child?"

Robert sighed, running a hand through his hair. "Isabella, you know I care about you. But this is the reality of the situation. We're not ready for a child. We're not married, my career is just taking off. This would ruin everything."

"Ruin everything for you, you mean," Isabella retorted, her voice laced with bitterness. "What about me? What about my dreams, my hopes for our future?"

"Your future is with me," Robert insisted. "We can still have a life together, a successful life. But not with a child. Not now."

Isabella stood up, her legs shaking with rage and heartbreak. "You're a monster," she said, her voice barely a whisper. "I never want to see you again."

She turned and fled the office, the sound of Robert's protests fading behind her. As she ran down the hallway, tears streamed down her face, each one a drop of poison, a reminder of the love she had lost and the betrayal she had suffered.

In that moment, Isabella knew she was alone. But she also

knew she was strong. She would survive this, she would raise her child, and she would never let anyone, not even Robert Bennett, dictate her future again.

The city lights blurred as Isabella stumbled down the sidewalk, her heels clicking a desperate rhythm on the pavement. The weight of Robert's words pressed down on her, a crushing burden of betrayal and despair. The tears she had held back in his office now flowed freely, hot and stinging, leaving streaks of mascara on her cheeks.

Each step felt like a betrayal, a physical manifestation of the emotional earthquake that had just shattered her world. The familiar streets of her city, once comforting and predictable, now seemed alien and hostile. She was lost, adrift in a sea of pain and uncertainty.

She found herself outside her family's home, the imposing structure looming over her like a silent judge. A flicker of hope ignited in her chest. Perhaps they would understand, perhaps they would offer her solace and support.

With trembling hands, she reached for the doorbell, but hesitated. The memory of her father's ultimatum, the cold finality in his eyes, flooded back to her. She couldn't face them, not like this, not broken and defeated.

With a sob, she turned away, her heels echoing her retreat. The city swallowed her up, its indifferent hum a stark contrast to the turmoil raging within her. She wandered aimlessly, seeking refuge in the anonymity of the crowd, her pain a raw, open wound.

The world became a blur of neon signs, car horns, and the chatter of strangers. Isabella felt like a ghost, drifting through the city, unseen and unheard. The weight of her isolation pressed down on her, a suffocating blanket of despair.

She found herself in a small park, a hidden oasis of green

amidst the urban sprawl. She sank onto a bench, her body wracked with sobs. The pain was a living thing, gnawing at her insides, tearing her apart.

How could he do this to her? How could he discard her, their child, so easily? The love she had felt for him, the dreams they had shared, now seemed like a cruel joke, a mirage in the desert of her despair.

As the night wore on, the tears subsided, leaving behind a hollow ache. Isabella stared up at the star-strewn sky, searching for answers, for a glimmer of hope. But all she found was a vast, indifferent universe, a stark reminder of her own insignificance.

She knew she couldn't stay here, wallowing in her grief. She had to find a way to move forward, to pick up the pieces of her shattered life. But how? Where could she go? Who could she turn to?

A flicker of determination ignited in her eyes. She wouldn't let this defeat her. She would find a way to survive, to thrive, to create a life for herself and her child. She would not let Robert Bennett's betrayal define her.

The world narrowed to the confines of her small apartment. The once vibrant colors seemed muted, the cheerful patterns on the wallpaper now a mocking reminder of the life she had envisioned. Isabella spent her days in a haze of morning sickness, fatigue, and a gnawing sense of dread.

Her once impeccable wardrobe lay untouched, replaced by loose-fitting dresses that couldn't quite conceal her growing belly. The mirror, once a friend, now reflected a stranger: a woman with swollen ankles, a puffy face, and eyes shadowed with exhaustion and worry.

The physical discomfort was nothing compared to the emotional turmoil that raged within her. The betrayal, the rejection, the loss - it was a heavy cloak that suffocated her spirit. Sleepless nights were filled with a jumble of anxieties: how would she provide for her child? How would she explain her situation to her friends and colleagues? How would she face the world alone?

The loneliness was a constant companion, a cold hand that gripped her heart. The silence of her apartment, once a sanctuary, now echoed with the absence of Robert's laughter, his whispered promises. The empty chair across from her at the dinner table was a stark reminder of her isolation.

But even in the darkest of hours, a flicker of defiance refused to be extinguished. It was a primal instinct, a mother's fierce love for the life growing inside her. Isabella would not be defeated. She would not let her circumstances dictate her fate.

She found strength in unexpected places. In the kindness of a neighbor who brought her a warm meal, in the encouraging words of a stranger she met at the prenatal clinic, in the gentle kicks of her unborn child that reminded her of the precious life she carried within her.

She found a part-time job at a local bookstore, a haven of words and stories that offered a welcome distraction from her worries. She started attending prenatal yoga classes, finding solace in the company of other expectant mothers and the gentle stretches that eased her aching body.

She poured her energy into preparing for her child's arrival, transforming her spare bedroom into a nursery filled with soft colors, cuddly toys, and the promise of new beginnings. With each brushstroke on the wall, each diaper folded and put away, Isabella felt a sense of purpose returning to her life.

As her body changed, Isabella struggled with her self-image. She missed the comfort of having someone to reassure her, to tell her she was beautiful. Instead, she started a ritual of positive self-talk, standing before the mirror each morning and finding something to compliment about herself and her growing bump.

The third trimester brought new challenges – swollen ankles, back pain, and increasing fatigue. Simple tasks became herculean efforts. There were days when just getting out of bed felt impossible. But Isabella persevered, reminding herself of the strong woman she was becoming for her child.

When labor finally began, Isabella faced her greatest fear – going through childbirth alone. But as contractions intensified, she found an inner well of strength she never knew existed. She focused on her breathing, on the encouragement of the nurses, on the thought of finally meeting her baby.

Hours passed in a blur of pain and determination. Just when Isabella felt she couldn't go on, the doctor announced it was time to push. With a primal cry, Isabella gave one final, monumental effort.

And then, piercing the air, came the sound she'd been waiting months to hear – her baby's first cry.

As the nurse placed the tiny, wriggling bundle on her chest, Isabella felt an overwhelming surge of love. Tears streamed down her face as she looked into her daughter's eyes for the first time.

"Hello, Evelyn," she whispered, her voice filled with awe. "We did it, little one. We're going to be okay."

In that moment, holding her daughter, all the struggles of the past months faded away. Isabella knew the road ahead would be challenging, but she also knew she had the strength to face whatever came their way. She had carried this life inside her, brought her into the world through sheer will and determination.

Isabella kissed Evelyn's forehead, making a silent vow. She would give this child all the love and support she deserved. And together, they would build a beautiful life, one day at a time.

The birth of Evelyn was a turning point, a moment of pure

joy that washed away the pain and fear. As she held her daughter in her arms, Isabella knew she had made the right choice. This tiny, perfect being was her reason for living, her inspiration to keep going.

Motherhood was not easy, especially as a single parent. There were sleepless nights, financial struggles, and the constant juggle of work and childcare. But Isabella found strength in the love she shared with her daughter, the unconditional bond that gave her life meaning.

She taught Evelyn about resilience, about the importance of independence, about the power of forgiveness. She showed her daughter that even in the face of adversity, it was possible to find joy, to create a life filled with love and purpose.

And as Evelyn grew, Isabella found herself growing too. She discovered a strength she never knew she possessed, a resilience that had been forged in the fires of betrayal and abandonment. She learned to forgive, not just Robert, but also herself, for the choices she had made.

The pain of the past never fully faded, but it became a part of her story, a chapter that shaped her into the woman she was today. Isabella's struggle had not been in vain. It had taught her the true meaning of love, the importance of family, and the unwavering strength of a mother's heart.

The years that followed were a study in contrasts. Isabella's life, once filled with promise and ambition, had become a relentless cycle of survival. Days bled into nights, each marked by the endless tasks of motherhood: late-night feedings, diaper changes, soothing a crying baby. The financial strain was constant, a gnawing worry that tugged at her every waking moment. She worked tirelessly, juggling multiple part-time jobs to make ends meet, her once manicured hands now roughened by housework and late-night sewing projects to make ends meet.

Meanwhile, Robert's star continued to rise. Newspaper headlines trumpeted his latest business ventures, his face gracing the covers of financial magazines. He was a regular fixture at high-profile events, his arm always linked with Katherine's, her perfectly coiffed hair and designer gowns a stark contrast to Isabella's worn-out sweaters and bargain-bin finds.

Isabella would catch glimpses of their seemingly perfect life in the society pages, a sharp pang of envy piercing her heart. She saw them laughing at a charity galas, their faces glowing with wealth and privilege. She read about their lavish vacations, their exclusive memberships, their ever-expanding social circle. It was a world away from her cramped apartment, where the constant hum of the refrigerator was her only company.

The injustice of it all was a bitter pill to swallow. While she struggled to put food on the table, Robert was dining in Michelin-starred restaurants. While she spent her nights comforting a sick child, he was attending black-tie events, his name whispered in awe by the city's elite.

The contrast between their lives was a constant reminder of what she had lost, of the future that had been stolen from her. It was a wound that refused to heal, a scar that throbbed with each new report of Robert's success.

But Isabella refused to let bitterness consume her. She found solace in her daughter's laughter, in the warmth of her embrace, in the small joys of everyday life. She taught Evelyn to appreciate the simple things: a shared meal, a walk in the park, a bedtime story read by candlelight.

Isabella's struggles had not extinguished her spirit. They had, in fact, ignited a fire within her, a determination to create a better life for herself and her daughter. She would not let Robert's betrayal define her. She would rise above it, stronger and more resilient than ever before.

Isabella's love for Evelyn was a beacon in the storm, a constant source of warmth and light in the face of adversity. It was in the gentle lullabies she sang as she rocked her daughter to sleep, the soothing touch of her hand on a feverish brow, the whispered words of encouragement in the face of childhood fears.

Evenings were spent reading fairy tales by the glow of a lamp, their laughter filling the small apartment with a warmth that money couldn't buy. Isabella made a game out of their meager meals, transforming plain rice and beans into a pirate's feast or a princess's banquet. She sewed costumes from scraps of fabric, turning their living room into a stage for impromptu plays where Evelyn was always the star.

Every milestone was a celebration. Evelyn's first steps, her first words, her first day of school – Isabella marked each occasion with handmade gifts, carefully crafted from recycled materials and overflowing with love.

When Evelyn struggled with her studies, Isabella was there, patiently explaining concepts, helping her with homework, and celebrating every small victory. When Evelyn felt lonely or scared, Isabella would hold her close, whispering stories of brave princesses and clever foxes, reminding her daughter of her own strength and resilience.

Even when money was tight, Isabella always found a way to make special occasions memorable. Birthdays were celebrated with homemade cakes and hand-drawn cards. Christmas mornings were filled with the magic of carefully wrapped gifts, each one a testament to Isabella's ingenuity and love.

Isabella's love for Evelyn was not just about providing for her material needs. It was about nurturing her spirit, fostering her creativity, and instilling in her a sense of self-worth that no amount of adversity could diminish. It was about showing her daughter that even in the face of hardship, love could bloom, joy could be found, and dreams could take flight.

The mirror in the bathroom reflected a stranger. Isabella hardly recognized the woman staring back at her. The once vibrant face was now gaunt, the skin stretched taut over prominent cheekbones. Her eyes, once sparkling with life, were now dull and hollow, framed by dark circles that spoke of sleepless nights and endless worry.

The years had not been kind. The constant struggle to make ends meet, the long hours juggling work and motherhood, the gnawing anxiety about the future - they had taken their toll on her body and spirit. She had always been slender, but now her clothes hung loosely on her frame, her bones protruding in a way that alarmed her.

She had ignored the persistent cough, the fatigue that wouldn't go away, the nagging pain in her chest. She had told herself it was just stress, just exhaustion, just a passing ailment. But deep down, she knew it was more than that.

The doctor's appointment confirmed her worst fears. The diagnosis was grim, the prognosis even worse. Isabella sat in the sterile examination room, her mind reeling. The doctor's words echoed in her ears, a death knell that shattered any illusions of recovery.

As she walked home, the world seemed to tilt on its axis. The familiar sights of her neighborhood blurred, the sounds of traffic fading into a distant hum. All she could hear was the doctor's voice, repeating the diagnosis, the prognosis, the limited options.

She thought of Evelyn, her bright, curious daughter, the light of her life. The thought of leaving her, of not being there to guide her, to protect her, filled her with a terror she had never known before.

That night, as she tucked Evelyn into bed, Isabella made a

decision. She would not let her illness be a secret, a burden her daughter had to bear alone. She would tell Evelyn the truth about her father, about the circumstances of her birth, about the love that had been lost and the betrayal that had followed.

It was time for Evelyn to know her story, to understand the sacrifices that had been made for her, to learn the truth about the man who had abandoned them both. It was time for Evelyn to know the full weight of her inheritance, the legacy of love and loss that had shaped her mother's life.

The dying embers of the fireplace cast long shadows across the living room, painting the walls with a warm, flickering glow. Isabella sat on the worn sofa, her daughter nestled beside her, their hands intertwined. Evelyn, now a bright-eyed teenager, looked up at her mother with a mixture of curiosity and concern.

"Mama, you've been acting strange lately," Evelyn said, her voice soft and hesitant. "Is everything alright?"

Isabella took a deep breath, her heart heavy with the weight of the truth she was about to reveal. "Evelyn sweetheart," she began, her voice barely a whisper, "there's something I need to tell you. Something I should have told you a long time ago."

Evelyn's eyes widened, her grip on her mother's hand tightening. "What is it, Mama?" she asked, her voice filled with a mixture of fear and anticipation.

Isabella took a moment to gather her thoughts, her gaze fixed on the dancing flames in the fireplace. "It's about your father," she said, her voice barely audible.

Evelyn's breath hitched. "My father?" she repeated, the word foreign and unfamiliar on her tongue.

Isabella nodded, her eyes filling with tears. "Your father... his name was Robert Bennett. He was a brilliant man, a charismatic businessman. We were... involved, for a time."

Evelyn listened, her mind racing to process this unexpected revelation. She had never known her father, had never even seen a picture of him. Her mother had always been evasive when it came to questions about her father, deflecting them with vague answers or a change of subject.

"But he left us," Isabella continued, her voice thick with emotion. "He abandoned us before you were born. He chose his ambition, his career, over you and me."

Evelyn's heart ached for her mother, for the pain she had carried for so long. "Why are you telling me this now?" she asked, her voice barely a whisper.

Isabella reached out, her hand cupping Evelyn's cheek. "Because I'm sick, my darling," she said, her voice choked with tears. "And I don't have much time left."

Evelyn gasped, her eyes widening with shock and disbelief. "No, Mama," she protested, her voice rising. "You can't leave me. You can't!"

Isabella pulled her daughter close, her arms wrapping around her in a fierce embrace. "I won't leave you, my darling," she whispered into Evelyn's hair. "I'll always be with you, in your heart, in your memories."

They sat there for a long time, mother and daughter, their bodies intertwined, their tears mingling. Isabella told Evelyn everything, about her love for Robert, about his betrayal, about the years of hardship and struggle.

Evelyn listened, her heart filled with a mixture of grief, anger, and a newfound understanding of her mother's life. She learned about the sacrifices Isabella had made, the strength she had shown, the love she had never wavered from.

As the night wore on, a sense of peace settled over them. The truth, once a hidden burden, was now a shared bond, a bridge between mother and daughter. Isabella had given Evelyn the gift of her story, a legacy of love and loss that would shape her daughter's future.

A knot tightened in Evelyn's chest, a cold fist clenching around her heart. Disbelief warred with a rising tide of anger, each word her mother spoke a fresh wound. This man, this stranger, was her father? The architect of their hardship, the reason for her mother's fading light?

"He abandoned us?" Evelyn's voice was barely a whisper, raw with hurt and confusion. The fairy tales she'd grown up with had always ended with a loving reunion, a father's return. But this story... this was a nightmare.

Isabella reached out, her frail hand finding Evelyn's. "Yes, my darling. He made his choice. A choice that left us to fend for ourselves."

Anger simmered in Evelyn's gut, a burning ember threatening to ignite. How could he? How could he discard them like yesterday's news, leaving them to scrape by while he lived a life of luxury? A life Evelyn had only glimpsed in the glossy pages of magazines her mother sometimes brought home from the bookstore where she worked.

"He has a family now," Isabella continued, her voice trembling. "A wife, children. A life you and I will never be a part of."

Betrayal twisted the knife in Evelyn's heart. Not only had he abandoned them, but he had replaced them. The unfairness of it all, the injustice, sent a fresh wave of anger surging through her.

"But why, Mama?" Evelyn cried, her voice thick with unshed tears. "Why did he leave us? Didn't he love you?"

Isabella's eyes filled with a bittersweet sorrow. "He did, once. But his ambition, his desire for power and success, it consumed him. He saw us as a burden, an obstacle to his grand plans."

The words were a poison, seeping into Evelyn's soul. She had always been proud of her mother's strength, her resilience in the face of adversity. But now, she saw the toll it had taken, the lines etched on her mother's face, the weariness in her eyes.

Grief mingled with the anger, a potent cocktail of emotions that threatened to overwhelm her. She wanted to scream, to rage, to tear the world apart. But she held it in, her anger hardening into a steely resolve.

"He will pay," Evelyn vowed, her voice low and determined. "He will answer for what he's done."

Isabella looked at her daughter, a flicker of alarm in her eyes. "Evelyn, no," she said, her voice weak but firm. "Don't let anger consume you. It will only destroy you."

But Evelyn was already lost in the darkness, her heart consumed by a thirst for justice, a hunger for revenge. Her father's betrayal had ignited a fire within her, a fire that would burn until he answered for his sins.

In the quiet of the night, as her mother slept fitfully, Evelyn's mind raced. A whirlwind of emotions swirled within her – grief for her mother's impending loss, anger at the injustice that had been done to them, and a fierce determination to right the wrongs of the past.

She sat by the window, the city lights a twinkling tapestry spread out before her. It was a world of privilege and excess, a world where Robert Bennett reigned supreme, oblivious to the pain he had inflicted on his own flesh and blood.

Evelyn's gaze hardened. She would not let him get away with it. She would make him pay, not just for abandoning them, but for every tear her mother had shed, every sacrifice she had made. It was a promise she made to herself, a vow whispered into the darkness.

But how? How could a girl from a modest background, a

girl with no connections or resources, bring down a man like Robert Bennett? The question gnawed at her, a puzzle she was determined to solve.

Days turned into nights, and still, Evelyn pondered. She spent hours at the library, poring over books and articles about corporate espionage, revenge plots, and the art of infiltration. She studied Robert Bennett's company, his business dealings, his vulnerabilities.

An idea began to take shape, a daring plan that would require cunning, patience, and a willingness to risk everything. She would infiltrate the Bennett household, not as Evelyn, the abandoned daughter, but as someone else entirely. Someone who could gain their trust, earn their confidence, and ultimately, expose their secrets.

She would become a housemaid.

It was a bold move, a gamble with potentially devastating consequences. But Evelyn knew it was her only chance to get close to Robert, to learn his secrets, to gather the evidence she needed to destroy him.

She spent weeks crafting her new identity, carefully constructing a backstory, a persona that would be both believable and unassuming. She practiced her accent, her mannerisms, her every move, until she could slip seamlessly into the role of a humble housemaid, her true intentions hidden beneath a mask of subservience.

The day she arrived at the Bennett estate, her heart pounding in her chest, Evelyn knew there was no turning back. As she stepped across the threshold, she left behind her old life, her true identity, everything that had once defined her.

She was no longer Evelyn, the abandoned daughter. She was now Evelyn, the housemaid, a silent observer, a cunning infiltrator, a woman on a mission.

As the first rays of dawn painted the sky a fiery orange, Evelyn stood on the doorstep of the Bennett estate, her suitcase clutched tightly in her hand. A flicker of doubt momentarily clouded her eyes, but it was quickly extinguished by the burning embers of her resolve.

"This is for you, Mama," she whispered, her voice barely audible. "I will not rest until justice is served."

+++

CHAPTER 1

The Arrival

Behind the Gates

The taxi rattled along the narrow country road, its headlights cutting through the thick fog that clung to the landscape like a shroud. I gripped the worn leather seat, my knuckles white as I fought to suppress the rising panic in my chest. Each jolt, each turn of the wheel, brought me closer to my destination, the imposing iron gates that guarded the Bennett estate.

The taxi slowed to a crawl, the tires crunching on the gravel driveway as we approached the gates. The driver, a gruff man with a weather-beaten face, cast a curious glance in my direction. "This it?" he asked, his voice rough with a hint of suspicion.

"Yes," I replied, my voice barely above a whisper. "This is it."

The gates swung open with a groan, revealing a long, winding driveway that disappeared into the darkness. The taxi surged forward, its headlights illuminating the manicured lawns and towering oak trees that lined the path. The air grew heavy with the scent of damp earth and blooming jasmine, a deceptive sweetness that masked the rot that lay beneath.

As we rounded a final bend, the Bennett mansion emerged from the shadows, a monstrous edifice of stone and glass that loomed over the landscape like a predator stalking its prey. Its sheer size and opulence were both intimidating and exhilarating. This was the heart of the beast, the den of the man who had destroyed my family, the man I had come to destroy.

The taxi pulled to a stop in front of the grand entrance, its marble steps gleaming in the moonlight. I paid the driver, my hand trembling as I handed him the crumpled bills. He eyed me curiously, a silent question hanging in the air. But I offered no explanation, no hint of the turmoil that raged within me.

I stepped out of the taxi, the cold night air a shock to my senses. I took a deep breath, steeling myself for the task ahead. I had spent months planning for this moment, meticulously crafting a new identity, a mask to conceal my true intentions. I was no longer , the grieving daughter seeking justice. I was now Miss Evelyn, a highly qualified housemaid with impeccable references and a charming demeanor.

I smoothed down my crisp white uniform, adjusted the pearl earrings that dangled from my ears, and plastered a polite smile on my face. It was time to begin the performance, to play the part of the innocent lamb entering the lion's den.

With my heart pounding in my chest, I approached the front door, my fingers tracing the intricate carvings on the heavy oak. As I reached for the brass knocker, a wave of doubt washed over me. Was I really ready for this? Could I really go through with my plan?

But the image of my mother's frail body, her sunken eyes filled with pain and regret, flashed before my eyes. It was a reminder of the injustice that had been done, the debt that needed to be repaid.

I took a deep breath, banishing the doubt from my mind. This was it. There was no turning back. With a trembling hand, I raised the knocker and let it fall, the sound echoing through the silent night like a death knell.

The taxi door clicked shut behind me, the sound echoing in

the sudden silence. I emerged from the vehicle, my heels sinking slightly into the manicured lawn as I took my first step onto the Bennett estate. The air was thick with the scent of blooming jasmine, a cloying sweetness that did little to mask the rising bile in my throat.

My heart hammered against my ribs, a relentless drumbeat that echoed the pounding in my head. This was it. The moment I had meticulously planned for, dreamt of, feared. Yet, as I stood before the sprawling mansion, a sense of unreality washed over me. Was this truly happening? Was I truly about to embark on this perilous path of deception and revenge?

I took a deep breath, the crisp night air a chilling reminder of the task ahead. I smoothed down my navy skirt, adjusting the crisp white blouse that hugged my torso. My hair, pulled back into a neat bun, not a strand out of place, framed my face, a carefully crafted mask of composure. My only adornment, a pair of pearl earrings, a gift from my mother, glinted in the moonlight, a silent testament to the pain and longing that fueled my every step.

The imposing facade of the Bennett mansion loomed before me, its windows dark and unwelcoming. A shiver ran down my spine, not from the cold, but from a chilling premonition of the darkness that lay within. This was a house of secrets, a place where the truth had been buried beneath layers of deceit and denial. And I was about to become a part of it.

I reached into my bag, pulling out a compact mirror. I stared at my reflection, the face of Evelyn, the woman I had become. Her eyes, once filled with warmth and laughter, now held a steely determination, a coldness that mirrored the iciness in my heart. This was the face of a woman on a mission, a woman who would stop at nothing to achieve her goals.

I took a deep breath, steeling myself for the task ahead. With one last glance at my reflection, I tucked the mirror back into my bag and turned towards the imposing front door. My steps were slow and deliberate, each footfall a declaration of intent. I was here. And I wouldn't rest until justice was served.

A chill wind whipped around me, a stark reminder of the chill that had settled permanently in my heart. I stood, frozen, clutching my worn leather suitcase – a stark contrast to the grandeur before me. The mansion was a silent beast, windows gleaming ominously like a predator's eyes in the moonlight.

The weight of it pressed upon me, the sheer opulence a slap in the face to the memory of my mother, wasting away in a cramped hospital bed. How dare they? I thought, bitterness twisting in my gut. How dare they live in such luxury while she suffers?

A surge of anger fueled my resolve. This was more than just a job, more than a paycheck. This was retribution. Every brick of this house, every manicured shrub, was a testament to their ill-gotten wealth, built on the back of my mother's misery.

As I gazed at the imposing structure, memories flickered through my mind like scenes from a horror film. My mother's hollowed cheeks, her trembling hand clutching mine as she recounted the tale of her betrayal. Robert Bennett, a name that had become synonymous with deceit and heartbreak.

The image of his smug face, his cold eyes devoid of remorse, fueled the fire that burned within me. I saw him in the shadows of the mansion, a lurking figure of privilege and power. I could almost hear his laughter echoing through the halls, a taunting reminder of his victory over my mother.

But the laughter would soon turn to ashes in his mouth.

I had bided my time, patiently plotting my revenge. For years, I had watched from afar, studying the Bennetts, learning their weaknesses, their vulnerabilities. I had infiltrated their lives, disguised as a harmless housemaid, a wolf in sheep's clothing.

Now, the time had come to strike. The clock was ticking, each passing day a reminder of my mother's fading health. I had one year, maybe less, to make them pay. To expose their secrets, to shatter their perfect facade, to destroy the empire they had built on a foundation of lies.

The heavy oak door swung inward, revealing a woman who was the embodiment of refined elegance. Katherine Bennett, with her perfectly coiffed blonde hair and impeccable designer dress, exuded an air of effortless grace that belied the unease swirling beneath the surface.

"Miss Evelyn, I presume?" she inquired, her voice a melodic blend of warmth and formality.

"Yes, Mrs. Bennett," I replied, offering a practiced smile. "Thank you so much for seeing me at such short notice."

Katherine gestured towards a plush armchair in the opulent sitting room, her eyes scanning me with a discerning gaze. I took a seat, my back ramrod straight, my hands folded neatly in my lap. I had anticipated this moment, meticulously preparing my responses, anticipating every possible question. But as I met Katherine's eyes, I couldn't shake the feeling that she was seeing through my carefully constructed facade.

"Your references were impeccable," Katherine remarked, her voice betraying a hint of skepticism. "But there's something...intangible...that I can't quite put my finger on."

I offered another practiced smile, my heart pounding in my chest. "I understand your hesitation, Mrs. Bennett. It's a big decision, entrusting your children to a stranger."

"Indeed," Katherine agreed, her eyes narrowing slightly. "And with everything that's been happening lately, we're especially cautious."

Her words sent a jolt of unease through me. Had she heard whispers of the scandal that had engulfed my previous employer? Had she somehow uncovered the truth about my past?

I met her gaze with feigned innocence. "I assure you, Mrs. Bennett, I'm fully qualified and capable of caring for your children. My references can attest to my experience and dedication."

Katherine nodded, but the skepticism in her eyes remained. She leaned forward, her voice dropping to a confidential tone. "Tell me, Miss Evelyn, why did you choose to apply for this position? It's not exactly a typical housemaid job."

I hesitated for a moment, carefully choosing my words. "I was drawn to the challenge," I replied, my voice steady. "I'm looking for a position that will allow me to utilize my skills and experience fully. And your family, with its unique needs and circumstances, seemed like a perfect fit."

Katherine studied me for a long moment, her eyes searching for any sign of deceit. But I held her gaze, my face a mask of sincerity. I had played this role before, and I knew how to convince even the most discerning observer.

After a moment, Katherine leaned back, a faint smile playing on her lips. "Very well, Miss Evelyn," she said. "I'm willing to give you a chance. But I must warn you, this family is not without its challenges."

I nodded, my heart pounding with a mixture of relief and anticipation. "I'm up for the challenge, Mrs. Bennett," I replied, my voice filled with feigned confidence. "I'm confident that I can meet your expectations."

Katherine's smile widened, but her eyes remained cold and calculating. I knew that this was just the beginning of a game of cat and mouse, a battle of wits between two women with their own hidden agendas. And as I rose to my feet, ready to begin my new role as the Bennett's housemaid, I knew that I had entered a world of danger and deception, a world where the line between truth and lies was blurred, and the consequences of my actions could be devastating. I could sense her wariness, her keen eyes searching for a crack in my facade. But I had honed my performance over years of practice, each smile, each gesture, a carefully calibrated weapon in my arsenal of deception.

Yet, as Katherine and I exchanged pleasantries, a prickling sensation at the back of my neck alerted me to another presence in the room. I turned my head ever so slightly, my peripheral vision catching a flicker of movement in the doorway. A young boy, no more than ten years old, stood half-hidden in the shadows, his eyes wide and unblinking as he observed the scene before him.

"Max, darling," Katherine chided, her voice taking on a saccharine sweetness. "Don't sneak up on people like that."

The boy stepped into the light, revealing a mop of unruly brown hair and a pair of eyes that sparkled with intelligence. He couldn't have been more than ten, but there was a wisdom in his gaze that belied his age. This was Max, the youngest Bennett, the one they often overlooked.

"Sorry, Mummy," he mumbled, his cheeks flushing with embarrassment. But his eyes remained fixed on me, taking in my every detail with the intensity of a seasoned detective.

I knelt down, meeting his gaze at eye level. "Hello, Max," I said, offering him a warm smile. "It's nice to meet you."

He tilted his head, studying me for a moment before responding. "You're the new housemaid, right?"

"That's right," I confirmed. "My name is Evelyn."

He nodded slowly, his eyes still narrowed in concentration. "You have a nice smile," he finally said, a hint of a shy grin tugging at his lips.

I felt a pang of guilt, a flicker of doubt. This boy, so innocent and trusting, was about to be caught in the crossfire of my vengeance. But I quickly pushed the thought aside. He was a

Bennett, and that meant he was fair game.

"Thank you, Max," I said, reaching out to ruffle his hair. "You have a nice smile too."

He ducked away, a mischievous glint in his eyes. "Don't do that," he said, a hint of laughter in his voice. "I'm not a baby."

"Of course not," I agreed, rising to my feet. "You're a big boy now."

He puffed out his chest, clearly pleased with the compliment. "I'm ten," he declared proudly. "And I'm going to be a scientist when I grow up."

"A scientist?" I echoed, impressed by his ambition. "That's very impressive."

He beamed, his eyes alight with excitement. "I'm going to invent all sorts of things," he continued, his words tumbling out in a rush. "Robots, and time machines, and maybe even a portal to another dimension."

I couldn't help but chuckle. "Well, Max," I said, "I look forward to seeing all your amazing inventions."

He grinned, his confidence infectious. "You will," he assured me. "I promise."

As we continued the tour, Max trailed after me, peppering me with questions about my life, my interests, my dreams. He was like a sponge, soaking up every detail, every nuance.

I answered his questions carefully, revealing just enough to satisfy his curiosity while keeping my true motives hidden. But even as I spoke, I couldn't shake the feeling that I was being observed, studied.

Max's eyes followed my every move, his young mind piecing together the puzzle of who I was and why I was here. He was a wildcard, a variable I hadn't accounted for. And as I looked into his bright, inquisitive eyes, I knew that he would be a force to be reckoned with.

As our eyes met, a shiver ran down my spine. There was something unsettling about his unwavering stare, a silent scrutiny that pierced through my carefully constructed facade. I quickly averted my gaze, returning my attention to Katherine.

The interview concluded shortly after, Katherine offering me a polite handshake and as I gathered my belongings and prepared to be showed to my room, I couldn't help but steal another glance at Max. He remained in the doorway, his small frame a silhouette against the dimly lit hallway. His eyes, fixed on my back.

As I walked away from the Bennett mansion, the weight of Max's gaze heavy upon me, I couldn't help but wonder what role he would play in the unfolding drama. Would he be the one to unravel my secrets, to expose my true intentions? Or would he, in his own quiet way, become an unwitting pawn in my game of revenge?

The tour continued, Katherine's heels clicking a staccato rhythm on the polished floors. We passed through a formal dining room, its long mahogany table a battlefield where unspoken tensions simmered. We glimpsed a library overflowing with leather-bound volumes, a testament to Robert's carefully cultivated image of intellectualism. And then, finally, the heart of the beast: his office.

"This is where Robert spends most of his time," Katherine said, her voice dropping to a hushed reverence as she opened the heavy oak door.

It was a room designed to intimidate, from the towering windows that offered a panoramic view of the meticulously manicured grounds to the massive desk that dominated the space. Behind it sat Robert Bennett himself, a man whose reputation preceded him.

He rose as we entered, a shark in a tailored suit. His eyes, the color of steel, swept over me with a predatory intensity that made my skin crawl.

"Evelyn, I presume?" he asked, his voice a gravelly baritone.

"Yes, Mr. Bennett," I replied, meeting his gaze head-on. "It's a pleasure to finally meet you."

He extended a hand, his grip firm, almost bruising. "The pleasure is mine," he said, his eyes lingering on my face a moment too long.

A wave of disgust washed over me, but I maintained my composure, my smile unwavering. This man, the architect of my mother's misery, the destroyer of her dreams, stood before me, oblivious to the storm brewing beneath my calm exterior.

"Robert," Katherine chided gently, "you're making Evelyn uncomfortable."

He released my hand, a smirk playing on his lips. "Apologies, Evelyn. I have a tendency to be... direct."

"No offense taken, Mr. Bennett," I said smoothly. "I appreciate honesty."

Katherine cleared her throat. "Well, then. Shall we continue the tour?"

We left Robert to his empire of lies and deceit, moving on to the children's rooms. Max's room was a whirlwind of toys and books, a reflection of his boundless curiosity. Olivia's, on the other hand, was a stark contrast, its minimalist decor hinting at the emptiness within.

As we toured the house, I made a point of asking questions, engaging Katherine in conversation. I wanted to learn as much as I could about this family, their vulnerabilities, their secrets.

Katherine, in turn, peppered me with questions about my

experience, my qualifications, my background. I answered carefully, weaving a tapestry of half-truths and carefully crafted lies.

The power dynamics were clear. I was the employee, the hired help. But beneath the surface, I knew that I held a different kind of power, a power born of knowledge and a thirst for justice.

As we concluded the tour, Katherine turned to me with a practiced smile. "Well, Evelyn, I believe that covers everything. If you have any questions, please don't hesitate to ask."

"Thank you, Mrs. Bennett," I said, my voice sincere. "I look forward to working with you."

The echoing click of my heels on the polished marble floors was the only sound as I followed Katherine Bennett through the sprawling mansion in our walk of introduction. It was a labyrinth of opulence, each room boasting high ceilings, ornate furnishings, and a carefully curated collection of priceless art. Yet, beneath the veneer of luxury, I sensed a palpable tension, a simmering discontent that permeated the very air.

"This is Olivia's room," Katherine announced, her voice tinged with a hint of resignation. She paused before the heavy oak door, her hand hovering over the ornate brass knob. "She's a bit of a... challenge," she added with a forced smile. "But I'm sure you'll find a way to connect with her."

I nodded, my heart quickening with anticipation. Olivia, the troubled teenage daughter, had been a key figure in my research. Her rebellious nature, her rumored struggles with addiction, had painted a portrait of vulnerability, a potential weak point in the Bennetts' seemingly impenetrable armor.

Katherine pushed open the door, revealing a room that was a stark contrast to the rest of the mansion. It was a chaotic mess of discarded clothing, empty soda cans, and crumpled sheets of paper. The walls were adorned with a jumble of posters, some depicting rock bands, others showcasing dark, disturbing imagery.

A figure lay sprawled across the unmade bed, a tangle of long, dark hair obscuring her face. She wore a pair of ripped jeans and a faded band t-shirt, her slender frame barely visible beneath the rumpled covers.

"Olivia," Katherine called out, her voice a mix of concern and irritation. "This is Miss Evelyn, your new housemaid. She'll be staying with us for a while."

The figure on the bed stirred, a groan escaping her lips. She rolled over, revealing a pale face with dark circles under her eyes. Her gaze met mine, her expression a mix of defiance and apathy.

"Whatever," she mumbled, turning her back to us.

Katherine sighed, her shoulders slumping in defeat. "I'll leave you two to get acquainted," she said, her voice heavy with disappointment. She cast a final glance at me, a silent plea for help in her eyes, before leaving the room.

I stood there for a moment, taking in the scene before me. The room was a reflection of Olivia's inner turmoil, a physical manifestation of the pain and anger that consumed her.

That night, on my way from returning dishes from dinner I have served the family, I noticed Olivia's door was open, I took my first tentative steps into Olivia's domain. The air was thick with the mingled scents of stale perfume and cigarette smoke, a stark contrast to the sterile freshness that permeated the rest of the mansion.

I surveyed the room, my eyes taking in the chaos that surrounded me. Clothes were strewn across the floor, a tangled mass of designer labels and ripped denim. Empty soda cans littered the surfaces, their sticky residue a testament to Olivia's disregard for cleanliness. A stack of books teetered precariously on the edge of a nightstand, their titles ranging from classic literature to trashy romance novels.

A sense of unease settled over me as I took in the scene. This was not the bedroom of a pampered teenager, but rather a refuge for a troubled soul. The walls, adorned with a haphazard collection of posters, seemed to scream of rebellion and angst. Images of rock stars with smudged eyeliner and defiant sneers glared down at me, their rebellious energy a stark contrast to the meticulously curated artwork that graced the rest of the mansion.

I moved towards the unmade bed, my footsteps muffled by the plush carpet. A crumpled duvet lay haphazardly across the mattress, a testament to Olivia's restless nights. As I reached out to smooth it down, a small, cylindrical object caught my eye.

It was a pill bottle, lying discarded on the floor beneath the bed. I bent down, my heart pounding with a mixture of disgust and anticipation. I picked up the bottle, its label partially obscured by a sticky residue. As I turned it over in my hands, the name on the label came into focus: Oxycodone.

A chill ran down my spine as I realized the implications of my discovery. Olivia, the seemingly carefree teenager, was battling a demon far more insidious than teenage angst. She was addicted to painkillers, a secret she had clearly been hiding from her family.

I traced the worn edges of the pill bottle with my fingertips, a cold sensation creeping up my arm. It was a tangible piece of the puzzle, a confirmation of the cracks I'd sensed in this seemingly flawless family portrait. Olivia, the rebellious daughter, was a pawn ripe for the taking.

As I placed the bottle back on the nightstand, a surge of power coursed through me. The thrill of the hunt, the anticipation of the game, ignited a spark in my eyes. I had a plan, a meticulously crafted strategy that would dismantle the Bennett's from within. Each member was a carefully chosen target, their vulnerabilities exposed, their secrets ripe for exploitation.

With Olivia as my first pawn, I would sow discord, plant seeds of doubt, and watch as their seemingly perfect lives unraveled. The house, with its grand facade and labyrinthine corridors, would become my battleground, a stage for my carefully orchestrated revenge.

But beneath the thrill, a chilling realization settled upon me. This was no longer just a game. It was a dangerous dance with darkness, a descent into a world of manipulation and deceit. The lines between right and wrong blurred, my heart hardening with each calculated move.

I glanced at the sleeping figure on the bed, her face pale and drawn in the dim light. A pang of guilt tugged at my conscience, but I quickly suppressed it. This was not the time for sentimentality.

I turned to leave, my eyes lingering on the pill bottle one last time. A sinister smile played on my lips as I whispered, "Sleep tight, Olivia. The game has just begun."

As I closed the door behind me, a wave of chilling anticipation washed over me. The house seemed to hold its breath, every creak of the floorboards, every whisper of the wind through the eaves, a harbinger of the chaos that was to come. The Bennetts had no idea what awaited them, the storm that was brewing beneath the calm surface of their lives.

CHAPTER 2

Settling In

With a practiced eye, I began my reconnaissance. I started with the obvious: the security cameras. There was one in the corner of the sitting area, its unblinking eye trained on the doorway. Another, more discreetly placed, was tucked into the floral arrangement on the bedside table. I made a mental note of their locations, calculating angles and blind spots.

Next, I turned my attention to the windows. They were large, offering a breathtaking view of the sprawling estate, but also a potential escape route. I tested the locks, finding them surprisingly flimsy. With the right tools, they could be easily bypassed.

I moved to the bathroom, examining the layout. A small window above the bathtub caught my attention. It was barely large enough to squeeze through, but it opened onto a narrow ledge that ran along the side of the house. With a bit of ingenuity, it could serve as an emergency exit.

Back in the bedroom, I opened the closet, running my fingers along the neatly hung clothes. A hidden compartment behind a panel caught my eye. Inside, I found a safe, its combination lock a tantalizing challenge. I resisted the urge to tamper with it, knowing that drawing attention to myself this early.

As I surveyed my surroundings, a sense of claustrophobia washed over me. This room, for all its luxury, was a trap. A beautiful, gilded cage designed to keep me confined, to keep me under control.

The Bennett's idea of "housemaid quarters" was, unsurprisingly, extravagant. A self-contained suite tucked away on the third floor, it boasted a plush king-sized bed, a sitting area adorned with tasteful antiques, and a marble bathroom that wouldn't have looked out of place in a five-star hotel. Floor-to-ceiling windows offered a panoramic view of the sprawling estate, the perfectly manicured lawns stretching out like a green carpet towards the distant treeline.

Yet, despite the opulence, a sense of isolation hung heavy in the air. It was a gilded cage, a luxurious prison cell. The heavy curtains, drawn against the setting sun, cast long shadows that danced on the walls, giving the room an eerie, almost spectral quality. The silence was deafening, broken only by the rhythmic ticking of a grandfather clock in the hallway.

I moved through the space, my footsteps muffled by the thick Persian rug. I ran my fingers along the smooth surfaces, noting the meticulous attention to detail – the hand-carved moldings, the crystal decanters filled with amber liquid, the fresh-cut flowers arranged in a delicate vase. It was all so perfectly curated, so meticulously controlled.

A shiver ran down my spine. This room was a reflection of the Bennett family itself – beautiful, flawless, but ultimately hollow. It was a facade, a carefully constructed illusion designed to conceal the rot that lay beneath the surface.

I opened the armoire, its polished wood gleaming under the soft light. Inside, I found a pristine array of uniforms – crisp white blouses, tailored skirts, and sensible shoes. A silent reminder of my role in this charade. The housemaid, the caregiver, the trusted confidante.

But I was no mere housemaid. I was a wolf in sheep's clothing, a serpent in this Eden. And this room, this gilded cage, was my lair.

I moved to the window, pushing aside the heavy curtains to

peer out into the gathering darkness. Below, the lights of the mansion twinkled like a constellation of stars, each window a portal into a world of secrets and lies.

This was my battleground, my theater of war. And I was ready to play my part.

Within days, I had the Bennett household running like a well-oiled machine. Every morning, I rose before dawn to prepare a breakfast spread fit for royalty: freshly squeezed juices, artisanal pastries from the bakery downtown, and perfectly poached eggs. I learned that Robert preferred his coffee black, no sugar, while Katherine favored a delicate Earl Grey with a splash of milk. I memorized their schedules, anticipating their needs before they even voiced them.

But my duties extended far beyond simply feeding and clothing them. I became a confidante, a sounding board, a silent observer of their lives. I listened patiently to Katherine's petty complaints about her husband's neglect, her subtle digs at his questionable business practices. I offered Olivia a shoulder to cry on, a sympathetic ear for her teenage angst and unspoken anxieties. I even managed to win over the stoic gardener, Mr. Davis, with my cheerful demeanor and genuine interest in her work.

All the while, I was gathering information, like a spider spinning a web. I learned about Robert's late-night meetings, his encrypted phone calls, his hidden safe behind the Van Gogh in his office. I discovered Olivia's secret stash of pills, her hushed conversations with a mysterious dealer. I even found a draft of Katherine's divorce papers, tucked away in a folder on her laptop.

With each piece of information, my plan solidified, my resolve hardened. I wasn't just a housemaid, a mere observer. I was a puppet master, pulling the strings, orchestrating the downfall of this family.

One afternoon, while preparing Max's after-school snack, I noticed a small, leather-bound journal lying on the kitchen counter. It was Katherine's, I recognized the delicate handwriting from her grocery lists. Curiosity piqued, I flipped it open, my eyes scanning the pages filled with her neat script.

A passage caught my eye: "I can't take it anymore. He's suffocating me, controlling me. I feel like a prisoner in my own home. I need to find a way out."

A slow smile spread across my face. Katherine, it seemed, was already contemplating an escape. This was a weakness I could exploit, a crack in the foundation I could widen.

Closing the journal, I returned it to its place on the counter, my heart racing with anticipation. The game was afoot.

Max, ever the curious observer, became my shadow. He trailed me through the house, his eyes fixed on me with an intensity that was both endearing and unnerving. He asked me endless questions, his young mind hungry for knowledge, for connection.

I found myself drawn to his innocence, his unwavering belief in the inherent goodness of people. He was a stark contrast to the rest of his family, a beacon of light in a house shrouded in darkness.

One afternoon, while I was helping him with his homework, he looked up at me with his big, brown eyes. "Evelyn," he asked, "why did you come to work for us?"

I paused, my pen hovering over his math worksheet. "Well, Max," I replied, choosing my words carefully, "I needed a job, and your family needed a housemaid. It seemed like a good fit."

He nodded, but I could tell he wasn't satisfied with my answer. "But why us?" he pressed. "There are lots of other families you could work for."

I smiled, reaching out to ruffle his hair. "I like your family, Max," I said. "You're all very interesting people."

He grinned, a dimple appearing in his cheek. "We are, aren't we?"

But even as he smiled, I could see a flicker of doubt in his eyes, a hint of suspicion. He was too smart, too perceptive, to be completely fooled by my act. He sensed that there was more to me than met the eye, a hidden layer that he couldn't quite grasp.

One evening, as I was tucking him into bed, he asked me another question. "Evelyn," he said, his voice barely a whisper, "are you hiding something from us?"

My heart skipped a beat. Had he discovered my secret? Had he found the pill bottle in Olivia's room?

I forced a chuckle, trying to sound casual. "What do you mean, Max?"

He hesitated, his eyes searching mine. "I don't know," he finally said, "I just feel like... there's something you're not telling us."

I smoothed his hair, a maternal gesture that felt both genuine and manipulative. "Max," I said softly, "everyone has secrets. It's part of what makes us human."

He nodded slowly, seemingly satisfied with my answer. But as I left his room, I couldn't shake the feeling that I hadn't completely assuaged his doubts. He was watching me, studying me, waiting for me to slip up perhaps.

The air crackled with forced pleasantries and simmering resentments as the Bennett family gathered for their annual portrait. A renowned photographer, flown in from New York, fussed over lighting and angles, his booming voice echoing through the grand foyer.

Katherine, draped in a designer gown the color of twilight,

at any instance Katherine would not, my fingers lingering on his neck, feeling the pulse thrumming beneath his skin. I smoothed Katherine's hair, catching a whiff of her expensive perfume, a scent that masked the stench of decay beneath the surface. I offered Olivia a reassuring smile, my eyes silently acknowledging the pain she tried so desperately to hide.

And when Max's gaze met mine, I saw a flicker of recognition, a shared understanding. He knew, on some level, that I was not what I seemed. That I was maybe an outsider, an observer, just like him.

The shutter clicked, capturing a moment frozen in time. But I knew that this image was just a snapshot, a fleeting illusion. The real story lay beneath the surface, a tangled web of secrets and lies waiting to be unraveled.

The following week, Katherine met her friend, Margaret, for their weekly lunch at the country club. Over delicate finger sandwiches and steaming cups of tea, Katherine found herself confiding her growing unease about me.

"There's just something... off about her," Katherine confessed, her voice barely above a whisper. "It's like she's always watching, always listening. And those eyes..." She shuddered, remembering the unnerving intensity of my gaze.

Margaret chuckled, patting Katherine's hand reassuringly. "Darling, you're being paranoid. She's just a housemaid, not a femme fatale from one of your novels."

Katherine sighed, a frustrated frown creasing her brow. "I know, I know," she admitted. "But there's something about her that just doesn't sit right with me."

She recounted the incident like when she observed me with the pill bottle in Olivia's room, the way I had so quickly deflected any questions about it. She described the uncanny way I seemed to anticipate their every need, the subtle manipulations I employed to maintain control over the household.

Margaret listened patiently, nodding sympathetically, but her expression remained unconvinced. "Katherine, darling," she said, her voice dripping with condescension, "you're letting your imagination run wild. You've always had a flair for the dramatic, haven't you?"

Katherine bristled at the dismissal, a flicker of anger sparking in her eyes. "This is different, Margaret," she insisted. "I can feel it in my gut. Something isn't right with that woman."

But Margaret remained unconvinced, dismissing Katherine's concerns as the product of an overactive imagination. She reminded Katherine of her privileged life, of her loving husband, her beautiful children, her sprawling mansion. "You have everything a woman could possibly want," she chided. "Stop looking for problems where there aren't any."

Katherine, feeling defeated and alone, reluctantly let the matter drop. But as she sipped her tea, a lingering doubt gnawed at her. She couldn't shake the feeling that something was amiss, that a storm was brewing beneath the seemingly calm surface of her life.

And deep down, she knew that Margaret was wrong. This wasn't just her imagination running wild. This was a real threat, a danger lurking in the shadows.

The question was, could she convince anyone else before it was too late?

the resemblance between Evelyn and the woman from her memory... it was all too much of a coincidence.

She rushed to Robert's bedroom, rummaging through her jewelry box until she found what she was looking for: a worn photograph of Robert and Isabella, taken years ago at a company picnic. She held the locket next to Isabella's image, her heart pounding in her chest.

The resemblance was undeniable. The same heart-shaped face, the same high cheekbones, the same piercing eyes. The locket had belonged to Isabella, Evelyn's mother.

Katherine sank onto her bed, her mind reeling. It all made sense now. My arrival, my uncanny ability to anticipate their needs, my seeming subtle manipulations... it was all part of a plan. A plan for revenge in the imagination.

She felt a wave of nausea wash over her. How could she have been so blind? She had invited a viper into her home, a wolf in sheep's clothing.

But why? What could Evelyn possibly want from us? She retorted.

Katherine's hands trembled as she clutched the locket, the weight of her discovery heavy in her heart. She needed answers, but confronting me directly seemed too risky. She decided to bide her time, to observe.

That evening, during dinner, Katherine watched me closely, her eyes searching for any sign of deceit or guilt. But I remained the picture of composure, my smile warm, my demeanor attentive.

When Max accidentally knocked over a glass of water, sending it shattering across the floor, I was the first to react. I swiftly knelt, gathering the shards of glass with practiced efficiency, all while soothing Max's apologies.

It was a small act of kindness, but it struck Katherine as calculated, a performance meant to solidify her position in the household. As I cleaned up the mess, Katherine noticed there was no locket dangling from my neck.

"Evelyn," Katherine said, her voice betraying a hint of suspicion, "I found a locket on the floor earlier. It looks like something you might wear."

I turned, my eyes widening in surprise. "Oh my goodness," I exclaimed, my hand flying to her chest. "It's gone! I've been looking for it everywhere."

I rushed over to Katherine, her eyes scanning the floor. "Did you pick it?" I asked, pointing to the locket in Katherine's hand.

Katherine nodded, her eyes locked on my face. "Yes," she said slowly, "it is."

My eyes filled with tears. "Thank you so much, Mrs. Bennett," she said, with a voice thick with emotion. "This locket belonged to my mother. It's one of the few things I have left of her."

Katherine's heart softened. She had been so caught up in her suspicions that she had forgotten Evelyn was grieving the loss of her mother.

"I'm so sorry for your loss," Katherine said gently, handing her the locket.

I took it, my fingers tracing the delicate engraving. "Thank you," I whispered, my eyes glistening with unshed tears. "It means the world to me."

For a moment, Katherine felt a pang of guilt. Perhaps she had misjudged me. Perhaps I was just a grieving young woman, trying to make a new life for herself.

But as I turned away, a flicker of triumph in her eyes, Katherine's doubts resurfaced. The performance was too perfect, the tears too calculated.

I had provided a plausible explanation, but the seeds of doubt had been sown. And Katherine knew, deep down, that the truth was far more sinister than she could ever imagine.

Katherine, unsettled by the locket incident, resolved to test my mettle. She wouldn't accuse me outright, not yet. But she would probe, push, and see how the young housemaid reacted under pressure.

The opportunity arose during a routine grocery shopping trip. As I carefully selected fresh produce, Katherine casually mentioned a change in Max's dietary restrictions.

"Dr. Miller suggested we eliminate dairy from Max's diet," Katherine stated, her voice nonchalant. "He seems to be developing a slight intolerance."

I paused, a flicker of surprise crossing her face. "Dairy? That's odd," I murmured, a thoughtful frown creasing my brow. "I haven't noticed any adverse reactions."

Katherine's heart quickened. Was this the opening she had been waiting for? A slip-up, a reveal of my inattentiveness?

"Well, perhaps you haven't been paying close enough attention," Katherine retorted, her voice sharper than intended. "I would appreciate it if you would follow the doctor's instructions."

I turned to face her, my expression a mask of polite concern. "Of course, Mrs. Bennett," I said smoothly. "I always prioritize the children's health and well-being. I'll make sure to adjust Max's meals accordingly."

Katherine studied me, searching for any hint of resentment or defiance. But my demeanor remained impeccable, my voice calm and reassuring.

"Thank you, Evelyn," Katherine said, her tone softening slightly. "I appreciate your understanding."

But the seeds of doubt had been sown. Katherine couldn't shake the feeling that I was hiding something, that her acquiescence was merely a facade.

The rest of the shopping trip passed in an uneasy silence, the tension between we two thick enough to cut with a knife. As we returned to the mansion, laden with bags of groceries, Katherine's mind raced.

She had expected me to bristle at the challenge, to reveal a hint of my true nature. But the housemaid had remained unflappable, her mask of perfection firmly in place.

Katherine realized that she may be dealing with a formidable opponent, a woman who was skilled at manipulation and deception.

Days turned into weeks, and my presence in the Bennett household became increasingly entrenched. I had seamlessly woven herself into the fabric of their lives, anticipating their needs, managing their schedules, and offering a comforting presence to each family member.

Katherine, however, remained vigilant, her suspicions simmering beneath the surface. She watched me with a keen eye, analyzing my every move, every word. She noticed the subtle ways in which I exerted my influence over the family, gently steering conversations, and subtly undermining most of her authority.

One afternoon, while I was reading to Max in the living room, Katherine decided to test me. She entered the room, her face a mask of concern.

"Evelyn," she said, her voice sharp, "I'm afraid I need to speak with Max for a moment. It's about his schoolwork."

I looked up, a polite smile gracing my lips. "Of course, Mrs. Bennett," I said, closing the book gently. "Max, why don't you go with your mother? We can finish the story later."

Max, his eyes wide with curiosity, looked from me to his mother and back again. Katherine held her breath, waiting for my reaction.

But I simply smiled, my eyes twinkling with amusement. "Don't worry, Max," she said, ruffling his hair. "We'll have plenty of time for stories later."

Max, reassured by my calm demeanor, reluctantly followed his mother out of the room. Katherine led him to the study, closing the door behind them.

"Max," she said, her voice stern, "I need you to tell me everything you know about Evelyn."

Max's eyes widened in surprise. "What do you mean, Mummy?" he asked, his voice barely a whisper.

Katherine knelt down, taking his hands in hers. "I'm worried about her, Max," she said, her voice trembling slightly. "I don't think she's who she says she is."

Max hesitated, his eyes darting nervously around the room. He didn't want to betray me, but he also didn't want to lie to his mother.

"I don't know what you mean, Mummy," he repeated, his voice barely audible.

Katherine sighed, her shoulders slumping in defeat. She knew she couldn't force Max to tell her anything he didn't want to.

"It's alright, darling," she said, pulling him into a hug. "I just want you to be careful. Promise me you'll tell me if anything seems strange or out of place."

Max nodded, his small arms wrapping around his mother's neck. "I promise, Mummy," he whispered.

Katherine held him close, her heart aching with worry. She knew I was playing a dangerous game, but she couldn't ignore her instincts. She had to find out the truth about me, no matter the cost.

Later that evening, as I was preparing for bed, I couldn't help but smile. Katherine's attempt to undermine me had been a feeble one, easily deflected. It only served to confirm Evelyn's suspicions that Katherine was on to her.

But I was not one to be underestimated. I have been playing this game for a while now, and I am beginning to master how to win. I would continue to play her part, to earn the family's trust, to lull them into a false sense of security.

And when the time was right, I would strike.

CHAPTER 4

Olivia's Struggle

Olivia's behavior grew increasingly erratic. She disappeared for hours on end, returning with bloodshot eyes and a vacant stare. Her appetite waned, her once vibrant personality fading into a shadow of its former self.

Evelyn, ever the observant housemaid, took notice of the changes. She saw the way Olivia flinched at sudden noises, the way she trembled when left alone. She heard the hushed whispers during Olivia's phone calls, the furtive exchanges of cash in the dead of night.

One afternoon, while cleaning Olivia's room, Evelyn stumbled upon a hidden stash of pill bottles tucked away in a hollowed-out book. The labels were torn off, but Evelyn recognized the telltale shapes and colors of prescription painkillers.

Her heart sank as she realized the extent of Olivia's addiction. This wasn't just a rebellious phase, a teenage experiment. This was a full-blown crisis, a life teetering on the edge of a precipice.

Evelyn knew she had a choice to make. She could expose Olivia's secret, alerting her parents to the danger their daughter was in. Or she could use this information to her advantage, exploiting Olivia's vulnerability to further her own agenda.

For a moment, a flicker of compassion stirred within her. Olivia was just a child, lost and alone, crying out for help. But the memory of her mother's suffering, the injustice that had been inflicted upon her family, quickly extinguished any sympathy Evelyn might have felt.

This was war, and in war, there were no innocent bystanders. Olivia was a Bennett, and that meant she was a casualty, a pawn in a game she didn't even know she was playing.

Evelyn carefully replaced the pill bottles, her mind racing. She saw in Olivia's addiction not just a weakness, but an opportunity. A way to infiltrate the heart of the Bennett family, to sow discord and distrust.

She would become Olivia's confidante, her protector, the one person she could rely on. She would gain her trust, her loyalty, her dependence.

Evelyn made it her mission to be a constant, comforting presence in Olivia's life. She brought her tea in bed, fluffed her pillows, and picked up the discarded clothes that littered her room without a word of judgment. She offered a listening ear, a shoulder to cry on, a safe space for Olivia to vent her frustrations and fears.

One evening, as Olivia sat hunched over her desk, a textbook open but untouched, Evelyn knocked gently on the door.

"Come in," Olivia mumbled, her voice muffled by her arms.

Evelyn entered, carrying a tray laden with steaming chamomile tea and a plate of cookies. "I thought you might need a break," she said, setting the tray down on the desk.

Olivia looked up, her eyes red-rimmed and swollen. "Thanks," she muttered, reaching for a cookie.

Evelyn sat down on the edge of the bed, her hands folded in her lap. "How are you feeling?" she asked, her voice soft and soothing.

Olivia shrugged, her gaze fixed on the cookie in her hand. "Same as always," she mumbled. "Like crap."

Evelyn nodded sympathetically. "I know it's hard," she said. "But you're not alone."

Olivia scoffed. "Easy for you to say," she retorted. "You don't know what it's like."

Evelyn leaned forward, her eyes locking with Olivia's. "Actually," she said, her voice barely a whisper, "I do."

Olivia's head snapped up, her eyes widening in surprise. "What?" she asked, her voice laced with suspicion.

Evelyn took a deep breath, summoning a flicker of pain into her eyes. "When I was younger," she began, her voice barely audible, "I lost someone very dear to me. Someone who was supposed to protect me, to keep me safe."

Olivia's defenses seemed to soften, her curiosity piqued. "What happened?" she asked, her voice barely a whisper.

Evelyn hesitated, as if reluctant to share her pain. But then, with a visible effort, she continued. "He abandoned me," she said, her voice cracking with emotion. "He left me to fend for myself, to deal with the aftermath of his mistakes."

Olivia listened intently, her own pain resonating with Evelyn's story. She had always felt abandoned by her father, neglected and unloved. Evelyn's words struck a chord, a deep, unspoken understanding.

As Evelyn continued to share her story, weaving a tapestry of lies and half-truths, Olivia found herself drawn in, her defenses crumbling. She opened up to Evelyn, sharing her own struggles, her fears, her darkest secrets.

Evelyn listened patiently, offering words of comfort and understanding. She validated Olivia's pain, her anger, her resentment. She made her feel seen, heard, and understood.

By the end of the night, a tentative bond had formed between them. Olivia saw in Evelyn a kindred spirit, someone who had suffered as she had suffered. She felt a connection to her, a trust that she had never felt with anyone else in her family.

Evelyn, for her part, had achieved her goal. She had gained Olivia's trust, her loyalty. She had become her confidante, her protector, the one person she could rely on.

And with that trust came power, a power that Evelyn intended to wield with devastating precision.

The revelation came in the form of a phone call. It was the headmistress of Olivia's prestigious private school, her voice strained with a carefully suppressed panic. Olivia had been found unconscious in the girl's bathroom, a syringe lying discarded beside her.

Robert slammed the phone down, his face contorted with rage. He stormed out of his office, a dark cloud of fury following in his wake.

Olivia, still groggy from the paramedics' ministrations, was sitting on the edge of her bed, her head in her hands. She looked up as her father burst into her room, his eyes blazing with a cold fury she had seen countless times before.

"What the hell is this?" he roared, throwing a plastic bag onto the bed. It landed with a sickening thud, its contents spilling out – syringes, vials, a small bag of white powder.

Olivia recoiled, her body trembling. "It's not what it looks like," she stammered, her voice barely a whisper.

Robert grabbed her by the shoulders, his grip bruising. "Don't lie to me!" he thundered. "I know what this is. You're a drug addict!"

Olivia flinched, her eyes welling up with tears. "I'm not," she whimpered, her voice barely audible. "I just... I needed something to help me..."

"Help you with what?" Robert demanded, his voice dripping with contempt. "Help you cope with the fact that you're a worthless, pathetic excuse for a daughter?"

Olivia's tears flowed freely now, her shoulders shaking with sobs. "Please, Dad," she begged. "Don't be angry. I'll stop, I promise."

But Robert was beyond reason. He saw in Olivia's addiction a reflection of his own failures, a stain on his carefully cultivated image.

"You've disgraced this family," he snarled, his voice venomous. "You're nothing but a junkie, a liability. I won't have you ruining everything I've worked for."

He pushed her away, his disgust palpable. "Get out of my sight," he ordered. "I don't want to see you until you've cleaned yourself up."

Olivia stumbled back, her legs collapsing beneath her. She curled up on the floor, her sobs echoing through the silent house.

Robert stormed out, slamming the door behind him. The sound reverberated through Olivia's shattered heart, a final punctuation mark on her father's condemnation.

She lay there for hours, her body wracked with sobs, her mind numb with despair. The weight of her father's words pressed down on her, suffocating her, crushing her spirit.

She was alone, abandoned, cast out. A pariah in her own home.

Evelyn stood outside Olivia's door, her hand hovering over the doorknob. She had heard the raised voices, the slamming door, the heart-wrenching sobs. She knew this was her moment, her chance to swoop in and offer solace, to solidify her position as Olivia's confidante.

Taking a deep breath, she gently opened the door, revealing the crumpled figure of Olivia on the floor. Evelyn's heart ached with a mix of genuine sympathy and calculated manipulation.

She knelt beside the distraught girl, her voice soft and

soothing. "Olivia, honey," she murmured, "let me help you up."

Olivia looked up, her eyes swollen and red. She hesitated for a moment, then accepted Evelyn's outstretched hand.

Evelyn helped her to her feet, guiding her to the bed. She sat beside Olivia, wrapping her arm around her trembling shoulders.

"I heard what happened," Evelyn said gently. "I'm so sorry."

Olivia buried her face in Evelyn's shoulder, her sobs wracking her body. "He hates me," she choked out. "He thinks I'm worthless."

Evelyn stroked her hair, her voice a soothing balm. "No, honey, he doesn't hate you. He's just... disappointed. He doesn't understand what you're going through."

Olivia pulled back, her eyes searching Evelyn's face. "You understand?" she asked, her voice a mixture of hope and disbelief.

Evelyn nodded, a sad smile on her lips. "I do," she said. "I've been through something similar. My mother... she struggled with her own demons."

Olivia's interest was piqued. She had never heard Evelyn speak of her mother before. "What happened?" she asked, her voice barely a whisper.

Evelyn hesitated, as if reluctant to share her pain. But then, with a visible effort, she began to speak of her mother's struggles with mental illness, of the stigma and isolation she faced.

She painted a picture of a woman misunderstood by her family, a woman who sought solace in substances to numb the pain. She spoke of the heartbreak, the betrayal, the feeling of being utterly alone in the world.

Olivia listened intently, her own experiences mirroring

Evelyn's words. She had never felt so seen, so understood.

Evelyn's words, carefully chosen and subtly manipulative, planted a seed of doubt in Olivia's mind. Perhaps her father didn't understand her, perhaps he was incapable of understanding her pain. Perhaps Evelyn, the outsider, the stranger, was the only one who truly saw her for who she was.

Evelyn continued to comfort Olivia, weaving a tapestry of shared suffering and unspoken understanding.

In the days that followed, Evelyn became Olivia's constant companion. She brought her meals to her room, helped her with her schoolwork, and even accompanied her on doctor-mandated visits to a therapist.

Evelyn, grew to knew how to play on Olivia's insecurities. She listened patiently to Olivia's rants about her parents, her school, her life. She nodded sympathetically as Olivia bemoaned her lack of friends, her feelings of isolation and loneliness.

"They don't get it," Olivia would say, her voice bitter. "They don't understand what it's like to be me."

"I know," Evelyn would reply, her voice soft and soothing. "They're so wrapped up in their own lives, their own problems. They don't see the pain you're in."

Evelyn's words, carefully chosen and expertly delivered, planted a seed of doubt in Olivia's mind. A seed that grew and blossomed into a full-blown conviction that her family didn't care about her, that they only saw her as a problem to be fixed, an embarrassment to be hidden away.

One evening, as they sat on Olivia's bed, watching a movie on her laptop, Evelyn broached the topic of Olivia's addiction.

"I know it's hard," Evelyn said, her voice barely a whisper. "But you're strong, Olivia. You can get through this."

Olivia snorted, a bitter laugh escaping her lips. "Yeah, right,"

THE HOUSEMAID IS THE ENEMY

she said, her voice laced with self-loathing. "I'm a screw-up, a junkie. I'll never be anything more."

Evelyn reached out, taking Olivia's hand in hers. "Don't say that," she chided gently. "You're so much more than that. You're smart, funny, beautiful..."

Olivia's eyes welled up with tears. "No one else thinks so," she whispered, her voice choked with emotion.

"I do," Evelyn said firmly, her eyes locking with Olivia's. "I see the real you, Olivia. The kind, compassionate, intelligent young woman you are beneath all this pain."

Olivia leaned into Evelyn's embrace, her sobs muffled against her shoulder. For the first time in a long time, she felt safe, protected, loved.

Evelyn held her close, her own eyes glittering with a mixture of triumph and satisfaction. She had done it. She had broken through Olivia's defenses, had forged a bond that was both real and manipulative.

Olivia was hers now, a pawn in her game, a weapon to be wielded against the Bennett family.

With Olivia firmly under her influence, Evelyn felt a surge of power. She had gained a foothold in the Bennett household, a secret ally who would do her bidding. Olivia, desperate for acceptance and validation, clung to Evelyn like a lifeline, her trust absolute and unwavering.

Evelyn now new how to exploit this newfound leverage. She subtly sowed seeds of discord between Olivia and her parents, whispering doubts and fueling resentments.

"They don't understand you, Olivia," she would murmur, as she brushed the girl's hair or helped her choose an outfit. "They're too caught up in their own problems to see the pain you're in."

Olivia, already disillusioned with her parents, readily absorbed Evelyn's words. She began to see her family through Evelyn's eyes, their flaws magnified, their love and concern dismissed as mere obligation.

Evelyn also used her influence over Olivia to gain access to information. She encouraged Olivia to confide in her, to share her secrets, her fears, her hopes. She learned about Robert's shady business dealings, Katherine's secret bank accounts, Max's growing suspicions.

With each piece of information, Evelyn's power grew. She was no longer just a housemaid, a mere observer. She was a player in the game, a force to be reckoned with.

One evening, as Evelyn tucked Olivia into bed, she noticed a flicker of hesitation in the girl's eyes.

"What is it, honey?" Evelyn asked, her voice soft and soothing.

Olivia bit her lip, her gaze fixed on the floor. "Do you think my parents really love me?" she asked, her voice barely a whisper.

Evelyn paused, carefully weighing her words. "Of course they love you, Olivia," she said, her voice filled with feigned sincerity. "They just have a funny way of showing it."

Olivia sighed, her shoulders slumping in defeat. "I guess," she murmured, turning away from Evelyn.

Evelyn smiled, a triumphant glint in her eyes. She had planted the seed of doubt, the seed of alienation. Olivia was no longer just a pawn in her game, she was a weapon, a tool to be used to dismantle the Bennett family from the inside out.

CHAPTER 5

Corporate Troubles

The gleaming façade of Bennett Enterprises was starting to show cracks. It began with a series of whispers, hushed conversations in the corridors of power, and furtive glances exchanged during board meetings. Then came the articles, buried deep within the financial section of the newspaper, hinting at irregularities, questionable accounting practices, and suspicious offshore transactions.

Robert, ever the master of appearances, dismissed the rumors as the jealous murmurings of his competitors. But beneath his bravado, a cold dread was beginning to take root. He knew, deep down, that the foundations of his empire were built on shaky ground.

One morning, as he sat in his opulent office, sipping his black coffee and scanning the headlines, a name jumped out at him: Medina Mitchell. A former employee, a disgruntled accountant who had been quietly laid off months ago. Now, she was speaking out, her voice a clarion call in the wilderness of corporate corruption.

Mitchell, in a series of anonymous interviews, detailed a pattern of financial malfeasance, a web of shell companies and offshore accounts designed to siphon off profits and evade taxes. She spoke of bribes, kickbacks, and shady deals made in smoke-filled rooms.

Robert's blood ran cold as he read her accusations. They were too specific, too detailed, to be dismissed as mere speculation. Mitchell had been on the inside, a witness to his carefully constructed house of cards.

He slammed his fist on the desk, the sound echoing through the silent room. "Find her," he growled to his assistant, his voice barely controlled. "Find her and silence her."

But it was too late. The damage had been done. The whispers had turned into a roar, the articles into front-page news. Investors were getting nervous, regulators were circling, and the once-unassailable Bennett empire was teetering on the brink.

Robert knew he was in a fight for his life, a fight he could not afford to lose. He had spent decades building his empire, sacrificing everything – his morals, his relationships, his very soul – for power and wealth. He would not let it all crumble now.

He reached for the phone, his fingers dialing a familiar number. "We need to talk," he said, his voice low and menacing. "It's about damage control."

The echoing clack of Robert's shoes on the marble was a constant irritant, a metronome marking the time until his inevitable downfall. I could practically feel the tension radiating from him as he paced, his empire crumbling around him. He was a caged animal, desperate and paranoid.

The city he once surveyed with pride now mocked him, each gleaming tower a monument to his greed and hubris. I could practically taste his fear, a bitter tang in the air. The silence of the night was broken only by the soft clink of my wedding ring against the countertop as I wiped, lost in thought.

The sudden clatter of glass nearly made me jump. Robert, startled and disheveled, stood before me, his eyes narrowed with suspicion. "What are you doing here?" he demanded, his voice raspy from lack of sleep.

I feigned surprise, turning to face him with a practiced smile. "Just tidying up, Mr. Bennett," I replied smoothly, my voice a soothing balm to his frayed nerves. "I couldn't sleep, so I thought

I'd make myself useful."

He scrutinized me, his gaze lingering on my face. I had always sensed a mixture of fascination and unease in his eyes, but now it was magnified, his paranoia turning me into a potential threat.

"Don't you ever sleep?" he asked, taking a long sip of his scotch.

"Not often, sir," I admitted with a hint of amusement. "I find that the night is when my mind is most active."

He grunted noncommittally, his eyes never leaving mine. I returned to my cleaning, my movements deliberate and calming. Perhaps I could be a temporary reprieve from the storm raging within him.

As he downed the rest of his scotch, I sensed a shift in his demeanor. The suspicion in his eyes gave way to a desperate plea for reassurance.

"Evelyn," he began, his voice barely a whisper. "Have you heard any... rumors lately? About the company, I mean."

I met his gaze, my expression carefully neutral. "Rumors, sir?" I echoed, feigning ignorance. "What kind of rumors?"

I knew exactly what kind of rumors he meant. The whispers of his misdeeds, the cracks in his carefully constructed facade. I was privy to more than he realized, a silent observer in the shadows. But I would play my part, the loyal and unsuspecting employee, until the time was right.

As Robert hesitated before me, uncertainty etched into every line of his face, I watched with careful calculation. He was a man accustomed to control, yet now he stood before me, vulnerable and searching for an anchor in the storm that threatened to engulf him.

When he finally spoke, his words hung in the air like a

confession. "Rumors of trouble," he admitted, his voice a mere whisper. "Rumors of... financial irregularities."

I maintained my composure, though inside, a surge of triumph pulsed through me. This was the moment I had patiently waited for—the crack in Robert Bennett's armor, the admission of his vulnerability.

"I see," I replied calmly, masking the flicker of interest that flashed across my face. It was crucial to tread carefully, to ensure I played the role he needed me to play—loyal, trustworthy, indispensable.

Robert leaned closer, his voice lowering to a conspiratorial tone. "I need to know if you've heard anything," he implored, his desperation palpable. "Anything at all."

I met his gaze squarely, holding his gaze with unwavering resolve. "I understand, sir," I assured him, my voice steady. "I'll keep my ears open."

As he turned to leave, a sliver of hope kindled in his eyes, I couldn't help but marvel at the irony of it all. Robert Bennett, the titan of industry, finding solace in the presence of his most underestimated adversary. Perhaps it was my outward display of loyalty that reassured him, or perhaps it was the illusion of control I offered amidst the chaos of his unraveling empire.

But for me, it was a strategic maneuver, a step closer to the culmination of my meticulously crafted plan. I would use this moment, this fragile bond of trust, to gather the information I needed, to ensure that when the time came, I would be the architect of his downfall.

Late one evening, as the house settled into a deceptive calm. Dinner had been a tense affair, Robert's unease casting a pall over the otherwise impeccable meal. The children had retreated to their rooms, leaving the adults to their own devices. Katherine, secluded in her study, poured over financial documents, her brow furrowed in concentration.

Under the pretense of dimming the lights for the night, I made my way towards Robert's office. The heavy oak door was slightly ajar, a sliver of light escaping into the hallway. The sound of Robert's voice, low and urgent, drew me closer.

I pressed my ear against the door, my heart pounding in my chest. Inside, Robert was on the phone with his lawyer, their conversation a hushed exchange of legal jargon and thinly veiled panic.

"The situation is dire," the lawyer's voice crackled through the line. "Mitchell's testimony is damning. We're looking at multiple lawsuits, potential criminal charges..."

Robert's response was a string of curses, his voice thick with rage and fear. "We have to stop her," he snarled. "Find a way to discredit her, to silence her. I don't care what it takes."

The lawyer hesitated. "It's not that simple, Robert," he said cautiously. "She has evidence, witnesses. We're fighting an uphill battle."

"Then find a steeper hill," Robert retorted. "I won't go down without a fight. I won't let that bitch destroy everything I've built."

I listened intently, my mind racing. The pieces of the puzzle were falling into place. Robert's empire was crumbling, his carefully constructed facade cracking under the weight of his own corruption.

A surge of adrenaline coursed through my veins. Silently, I retreated from the door, my thoughts ablaze with possibilities. Robert's desperation, his readiness to do anything to protect his empire, presented a unique opportunity. I could use this crisis to my advantage, to expedite his downfall, to bring about his ultimate ruin.

Robert's desperate whispers echoed in my mind, each syllable a piece of ammunition. His fear was palpable, his facade crumbling like the empire he had built on shifting sands. I saw the hunted look in his eyes, the way he flinched at every ringing phone, every headline. The once-powerful predator was now prey, his predatory instincts blunted by the stench of his own impending doom.

Knowledge was power, and I held a treasure trove of it. The secrets I had gleaned, the whispered conversations, the hushed exchanges, painted a damning picture of the Bennett family's dark underbelly. Bribes, illicit dealings, a labyrinth of offshore accounts—it was all there, ripe for the picking.

I could almost taste the bitter sweetness of revenge, the intoxicating thrill of watching the mighty fall. I imagined the headlines, the scandal that would rip through the Bennett empire, leaving it in tatters. Their name, once synonymous with power and wealth, would become synonymous with corruption and disgrace.

But patience was key. I wouldn't rush in blindly, like a fool. I would be a spider, weaving a web of calculated moves, each strand a carefully crafted manipulation.

Katherine, with her brittle pride, would be easy to unsettle. A few well-placed hints, a veiled threat here and there, would sow seeds of doubt and suspicion. Olivia, already teetering on the edge, was a volatile element waiting to explode. I would subtly fan the flames of her rebellion, pushing her towards self-destruction.

Even young Max, with his innocent curiosity, could be an unwitting pawn in my game. By gaining his trust, I could glean valuable information about his father's shady dealings.

I would be the silent puppeteer, pulling the strings, orchestrating the downfall of the Bennett empire from the shadows. As the storm clouds gathered, I knew my time would come. The Bennetts would fall, and I would be there to witness it, to savor the bitter triumph of vengeance.

The air in the Bennett mansion was thick with the aroma of lilies and the faint metallic tang of wealth. It was a facade that masked the turmoil brewing beneath the surface, a storm gathering momentum with each passing day. I, Evelyn, was not just an observer in this lavish drama—I was a player, carefully orchestrating the downfall of those who had wronged my mother.

One afternoon, as I meticulously polished the silver in the dining room, Katherine swept in, her demeanor tense and guarded. The phone call she took revealed snippets of her plans, plans that hinted at escape from Robert's grip. My heart quickened with anticipation. Was Katherine finally making her move, or was this just another illusion of hope?

I feigned indifference as Katherine informed me of her upcoming "business trip," a thinly veiled excuse to distance herself from the turmoil brewing at home. "Of course, Mrs. Bennett," I replied with practiced composure. "Is there anything I can do to help prepare?"

Her response was curt, a facade of control that barely masked her underlying unease. Katherine sensed the tension between us, the unspoken knowledge that I was a threat lurking in the shadows of their once-perfect world. I reveled in this silent battle of wits, knowing that each move brought me closer to my ultimate goal.

As Katherine readied herself for departure, I intensified my efforts. I observed Robert's unraveling psyche, witnessed firsthand the cracks appearing in his meticulously crafted facade. The whispers of financial irregularities and impending investigations fed the storm brewing around him, a storm I had carefully seeded.

One evening, while serving dinner, I overheard Robert's

heated conversation with his lawyer. His rage was palpable, his desperation evident as he demanded a cover-up of the brewing scandals. I suppressed a smirk. The Bennett empire was beginning to crumble, and I held the hammer poised to strike the final blow.

Later, in the solitude of my room, I clutched a worn photograph of my mother—a poignant reminder of why I had embarked on this mission of vengeance. "Soon, Mother," I whispered, tracing her smiling face. "Soon, justice will be served."

The memory of my mother's suffering fueled my determination. The Bennetts had inflicted irreparable harm upon her, and now, they would face the consequences. I was no longer just Evelyn, the quiet presence in their opulent home —I would an architect of their downfall, and I relished every moment leading up to their inevitable reckoning.

The mansion hummed with an electric tension the following day, as if every corner held whispered secrets and unspoken intentions. Katherine, moving with an almost spectral grace, seemed haunted by invisible specters. From my vantage point in the shadows, I observed her closely—the tightness around her mouth, the restless flicker in her eyes betraying her inner turmoil and desperation for escape.

As I meticulously dusted the grand piano in the music room, my eyes caught sight of a small, leather-bound notebook concealed beneath a stack of sheet music. Intrigued, I reached for it, feeling the smooth texture of its cover under my fingertips. It was Katherine's diary—a treasure trove of her deepest fears and vulnerabilities, waiting to be uncovered.

Retreating to the sanctuary of my room, I opened the diary with a mix of excitement and trepidation. Katherine's words painted a poignant picture of a woman suffocating in a life of privilege, shackled by the expectations of high society and a loveless marriage. Her entries revealed a soul yearning for freedom, for a life untethered from Robert's suffocating control.

As I opened deeper into the diary, a plan began to crystallize in my mind—a plan to exploit Katherine's discontent and hasten her separation from Robert. The diary was my weapon, a potent tool to manipulate and shape the course of their unraveling marriage. Yet, amidst my scheming, a pang of empathy tugged at my conscience. Behind the mask of privilege and wealth, Katherine was a woman trapped, much like my mother had been.

In the days that followed, armed with the knowledge gleaned from the diary, I subtly planted seeds of doubt and discontent. I orchestrated chance encounters and whispered insinuations, carefully stoking the flames of Katherine's growing resentment towards Robert. I watched with a mixture of satisfaction and guilt as her determination to break free intensified, her resolve hardening with each passing day.

The tension within the Bennett household escalated to a fever pitch. Robert, sensing Katherine's withdrawal, became increasingly controlling and suspicious. His once-charming facade cracked under the weight of his paranoia, exacerbated by the mounting corporate troubles besieging his empire.

In this tumultuous arena, I, the seemingly inconspicuous housemaid, assumed the role of a silent puppet master. My actions, driven by a relentless thirst for vengeance, propelled the family towards an inevitable breaking point, heedless of the potential repercussions.

CHAPTER 6

Max's Discovery

Young Max, often overlooked and underestimated, possessed a keen eye and an insatiable curiosity. He was a silent observer, a collector of information, always on the lookout for clues that might unravel the mysteries surrounding his family and their enigmatic housemaid, Evelyn.

One afternoon, while Evelyn was busy preparing tea in the kitchen, Max found himself drawn to her room, a forbidden territory that beckoned with the promise of hidden truths. With a mischievous grin, he slipped past the door, his small frame easily navigating the dimly lit hallway.

Evelyn's room was sparsely decorated, a stark contrast to the opulent surroundings of the rest of the mansion. A single bed, a small wooden desk, and a worn armchair were the only furnishings. But it was the contents of the desk drawer that caught Max's attention.

As he carefully opened the drawer, his eyes widened with surprise. Inside, nestled amongst neatly folded clothes, was a small wooden box. Max's excitement reached for the box, his fingers brushing against the cool metal clasp. With a click, the box sprang open, revealing its hidden treasures.

The first thing Max saw was a photograph of a young woman with kind eyes and a warm smile. It was Evelyn's mother. Max had never seen her before, but he felt a strange connection to her, a sense of familiarity that he couldn't explain.

Beneath the photograph was a stack of newspaper clippings,

each one detailing a scandal or controversy involving the Bennett family. There were articles about Robert's shady business dealings, Katherine's rumored infidelities, and Olivia's struggles with addiction. Max's mind reeled as he pieced together the fragments of information, his suspicions about Evelyn growing with each passing moment.

Why would Evelyn have these clippings? What was her connection to his family? And who was the woman in the photograph? These questions swirled in Max's mind, fueling his determination to uncover the truth.

With trembling hands, Max carefully placed the contents back in the box, his mind racing with possibilities. He knew that he couldn't tell anyone about his discovery, not yet. He needed to gather more evidence, to connect the dots and expose Evelyn's true motives.

As he crept out of the room, a sense of unease settled over him. He had stumbled upon a secret, a secret that could potentially shatter the fragile foundations of his family. But Max was no longer the naive child he once was. He was a detective, a seeker of truth, and he would not rest until he had uncovered the secrets that lay hidden within the walls of the Bennett mansion.

As I entered my room, a chill ran down my spine. The wooden box lay open on the desk, its contents exposed like a raw nerve. My heart hammered in my chest as I quickly surveyed the scene. The photograph of my mother was slightly askew, and the newspaper clippings were out of order. Someone had been here.

A wave of anger washed over me, but it was quickly replaced by a cold, calculating calm. I knew who the culprit was. Max. His curiosity was both a blessing and a curse. He was perceptive, intelligent beyond his years, but his meddling could jeopardize everything.

I heard the soft padding of footsteps approaching my door. I quickly closed the box, tucking it back into the drawer and smoothing out the covers of my bed. The door creaked open, and Max stood there, his face a mask of innocence.

"Evelyn?" he asked, his voice barely a whisper. "Are you busy?"

I turned to him, plastering a warm smile on my face. "Not at all, Max. Come in."

He hesitated for a moment, then stepped into the room, his eyes darting around nervously. "I...I was just wondering if you needed any help with anything," he stammered.

I could see the guilt etched on his face, but I decided to play along. "That's very kind of you, Max. But I'm quite alright. Just finishing up some chores."

He nodded, but his eyes remained fixed on the desk drawer. I knew he was dying to ask about the box, but he was too afraid to confront me directly.

"Is something wrong, Max?" I asked, feigning concern. "You seem a little troubled."

He looked up, startled. "Oh, it's nothing," he mumbled, quickly averting his gaze.

I knew I had to tread carefully. I couldn't risk alienating him, but I also couldn't allow him to uncover my secrets. "Max," I said softly, "I know you're a curious boy. It's one of the things I admire about you."

He looked up at me, his eyes wide with surprise. "Really?"

I nodded. "Yes, but sometimes curiosity can lead us down paths we might not be ready for. It's important to be careful, to trust your instincts, and to know when to ask for help."

His face softened, and I could see a glimmer of understanding in his eyes. "I understand," he said quietly.

I reached out and placed my hand on his shoulder. "I'm here for you, Max," I said. "If you ever have any questions or concerns, you can always come to me."

He smiled, a genuine smile that warmed my heart. "Thanks, Evelyn."

He turned to leave, but then hesitated, turning back to me. "Evelyn?"

"Yes, Max?"

"That photograph on ..."

My heart skipped a beat. "Yes?"

"Who is she?"

I took a deep breath, summoning all my composure. "That's my mother," I replied, my voice barely above a whisper. "She passed away a few years ago."

Max's face fell, and a look of sadness washed over him. "I'm sorry," he said softly.

I smiled sadly. "Thank you, Max" injecting my voice with a wistful longing that I hoped would tug at his heartstrings. "From afar, of course. She worked as a seamstress, I paused, allowing my words to settle into the space between us. Max's eyes, wide and earnest, never left my face. He was rapt, hanging onto my every word like a lifeline. The perfect audience.

"She kept those clippings," I continued, gesturing towards the box, "as a reminder of a world she could only dream of. A world where kindness and generosity reigned, where people like the Bennetts made a difference."

My voice wavered slightly, a carefully crafted tremor of emotion. I watched as Max's expression softened, his suspicion replaced by a tender empathy. He was buying it, hook, line, and sinker.

"She always hoped that one day," I said, my voice barely above a whisper, "I would have the opportunity to experience that world for myself. To be a part of something bigger, something meaningful."

I reached out and gently squeezed Max's shoulder, my touch lingering for a moment longer than necessary. "And now, thanks to you and your family."

Max's eyes glistened with unshed tears. He reached out and took my hand in his, his small fingers gripping mine tightly. "I'm glad," he whispered, his voice thick with emotion.

He nodded, then turned and left the room, closing the door softly behind him. I let out a sigh of relief, my heart still pounding in my chest. I had managed to deflect his questions, but I knew that this was just the beginning. Max was not easily fooled, and I would have to be even more careful in the future.

Max's youthful face, a canvas of curiosity and budding suspicion held my gaze for a beat too long. The moment stretched, a silent battle of wills playing out in the sterile confines of my room.

As he left my room, a sense of relief washed over me. I had successfully manipulated Max's emotions, using his innocence. I had turned a potential threat into an unwitting ally, a pawn in my game of revenge.

But as I watched him walk away, a pang of guilt gnawed at my conscience. Was I becoming the very thing I despised? Was I sacrificing my own humanity in pursuit of vengeance? These questions haunted me, their answers elusive and unsettling.

I knew that my path was fraught with moral ambiguity, but I could not turn back. The seeds of revenge had been sown, and now I had to reap the harvest, no matter the cost.

The opulent dining room, once a stage for elegant family dinners and lively conversations, now echoed with the bitter taste of marital discord. Robert and Katherine sat at opposite ends of the mahogany table, their faces etched with years of unspoken grievances and simmering resentment.

"You've been distant lately," Robert began, his voice low and accusatory. "Is there something you're not telling me?"

Katherine met his gaze, her eyes flashing with defiance. "Why should I tell you anything?" she retorted. "You never listen anyway."

"Don't be ridiculous," Robert snapped, his patience wearing thin. "I'm your husband. We're supposed to share our lives, our concerns."

"We used to," Katherine said, her voice laced with sarcasm. "But that was before you became obsessed with your work, before you started shutting me out."

"Obsessed?" Robert scoffed. "I'm providing for this family, for you! Don't you realize the sacrifices I make?"

"Sacrifices?" Katherine laughed bitterly. "You call spending all your time at the office and neglecting your family a sacrifice? You've turned this house into a mausoleum, Robert. A gilded cage where I'm expected to smile and pretend everything is perfect."

"Perfect?" Robert's voice rose, his anger barely contained. "Is that what you think? That everything is perfect? Do you have any idea what I'm going through? The pressure, the scrutiny, the constant threat of ruin? And yet you sit here, complaining about your trivial problems."

Katherine stood up, her chair scraping against the marble floor. "My problems are not trivial, Robert," she hissed. "I'm suffocating in this marriage, in this life. I feel like I'm drowning, and you're not even throwing me a lifeline."

"Don't be dramatic, Katherine," Robert said, his voice dripping with disdain. "You have everything you could ever want. A beautiful home, a loving family, a life most people would envy."

"Envy?" Katherine's voice cracked. "You think people envy me? They pity me, Robert. They see me as a trophy wife, a hollow shell of a woman with nothing to offer but her looks."

Robert's face hardened, his jaw clenched tight. "You're being ungrateful, Katherine. You don't appreciate what you have."

"And you don't appreciate me," Katherine retorted, her voice trembling with rage. "You never have."

The argument escalated, their voices rising and falling in a symphony of accusation and recrimination. Plates rattled, glasses clinked, and the air throbbed with the intensity of their emotions.

I stood in the doorway, watching the scene unfold with a mixture of satisfaction and unease. This was exactly what I had hoped for, a complete breakdown of their marriage. But I couldn't help but feel a pang of pity for Katherine, for the woman trapped in a loveless union.

As the argument reached its crescendo, I slipped away unnoticed, leaving the couple to their bitter dance of destruction. I knew that this was just the beginning of the end, the first crack in the facade of their perfect life. And I would be there to witness every moment of their downfall.

The echoes of the argument reverberated through the house, a chilling soundtrack to the disintegration of a family. Unseen, Max peered from the shadows of the hallway, his small frame trembling as he witnessed the raw, unfiltered emotions that ripped through his parents.

He had always perceived his parents as pillars of strength, the embodiment of love and stability. But the scene unfolding before him shattered that illusion, revealing the ugly truth beneath the polished veneer.

Robert's face, twisted with rage, spat out venomous words that cut deep. Katherine, her eyes blazing with defiance, retaliated with cutting remarks that exposed years of pent-up frustration and resentment.

Max watched in horror as his parents tore each other apart, their love replaced by a toxic cocktail of anger, hurt, and betrayal. He felt a knot tighten in his stomach, a mixture of nausea and despair.

The illusion of a happy family, carefully crafted and maintained for so long, was crumbling before his eyes. The pillars of his childhood were collapsing, leaving him feeling lost and alone.

He retreated to his room, the echoes of his parents' fight ringing in his ears. He curled up on his bed, tears welling up in his eyes. He felt betrayed, abandoned, and utterly disillusioned.

The world he had known, the world where his parents were the unwavering foundation of his life, no longer existed. In its place was a harsh reality, a reality where love could turn to hate, where trust could be shattered, and where the people you loved the most could become strangers.

As he lay there, his heart heavy with sorrow, a new resolve began to grow within him. He would no longer be a passive observer, a pawn in his parents' game. He would take control of his own destiny, find his own path, and create a life that was truly his own.

And in the midst of his despair, a glimmer of hope emerged. He remembered the kindness and compassion Evelyn had shown him, the way she had listened to him and offered him solace.

Perhaps, he thought, she was the one person he could trust, the one person who could help him navigate the treacherous waters of his family's demise.

He wiped away his tears, a newfound determination in his eyes. He would not let his parents' mistakes define him. He would rise above the ashes of their broken marriage and forge his own path, a path guided by truth, compassion, and the unwavering belief in a better future.

CHAPTER 7

The Investigator

The rhythmic ticking of the grandfather clock in the foyer was the only sound that dared to break the tense silence that had settled over the Bennett mansion. Each tick resonated with an ominous undertone, a foreboding prelude to the storm that was about to engulf the family.

A sharp rap on the heavy oak door shattered the tranquility. I exchanged a nervous glance with Katherine, who stood frozen by the staircase, her face pale and drawn. Robert, his brow furrowed in irritation, rose from his armchair and strode towards the door, his every step radiating authority and barely concealed anxiety.

As he opened the door, a figure emerged from the shadows of the porch. A man, tall and lean, with sharp eyes that seemed to pierce through the facade of composure Robert wore like a mask. He introduced himself as Detective Thomas Harrison, his voice a gravelly baritone that commanded attention.

"Mr. Bennett," he said, his tone clipped and professional, "I'm here to ask you some questions regarding your business dealings."

Robert's jaw tightened, his eyes narrowing with suspicion. "What business is it of yours?" he asked, his voice laced with barely suppressed hostility.

"I'm investigating a series of financial irregularities," Detective Harrison replied, unfazed by Robert's hostility. "I believe your company may be involved."

A cold shiver ran down my spine. The investigator's arrival was unexpected, a wrench thrown into the delicate machinations of my plan. I had anticipated a confrontation with Robert, but not like this. Not with an outsider prying into the family's secrets.

As Robert reluctantly invited the detective into the house, I retreated to the shadows, my mind racing with possibilities. How much did the investigator know? Was he a threat to my carefully crafted scheme? I had to find out, and quickly.

I watched as Robert led Detective Harrison into the library, the heavy door closing behind them with a resounding thud. I could hear the muffled sound of their voices, the occasional raised tone betraying the tension that simmered beneath the surface.

I knew I had to act. I had to protect my secrets, my identity, and my mission. But I also couldn't allow the investigator to unravel the web of lies that held the Bennett family together. I was caught between two opposing forces, a double agent forced to play both sides of the game.

With a deep breath, I made my way towards the library, my steps light and silent. I pressed my ear against the door, straining to hear the conversation within.

"... offshore accounts...tax evasion... insider trading..."

The words were like daggers, piercing the veil of secrecy that surrounded the Bennett empire. I felt a surge of adrenaline, a mix of fear and excitement.

A plan formed in my mind, swift and decisive. I knew I couldn't let the investigator get too close to the truth. With a deep breath, I smoothed down my apron, composed my features into an expression of innocent concern, and stepped into the hallway.

"Mr. Bennett," I called out, my voice laced with just the right amount of worry. "There's a phone call for you. It seems urgent."

Robert emerged from the library, his face etched with frustration and a hint of panic. He shot me a grateful look before following me to the study.

"Thank you, Evelyn," he murmured as he picked up the receiver.

I nodded and made my way towards the library, where the investigator sat alone, his eyes scanning the shelves lined with leather-bound books. I knocked gently on the door frame, a demure smile on my lips.

"Detective Harrison?" I inquired, my voice soft and polite. "Can I offer you some tea?"

He looked up, startled, and then a wry smile spread across his face. "That would be lovely, thank you."

I busied myself with the tea tray, my mind racing as I considered my options. I had to distract him, to divert his attention away from the incriminating documents that surely lay scattered across Robert's desk.

"I couldn't help but overhear your conversation with Mr. Bennett," I said, pouring the tea with a steady hand. "It sounds like he's in quite a bit of trouble."

The investigator's eyes narrowed. "Indeed," he replied, taking a sip of tea. "But I'm sure he'll be able to clear his name."

"Of course," I said, a hint of skepticism in my voice. "He's a very resourceful man."

We engaged in small talk, discussing the weather, the house, and the Bennetts' philanthropic endeavors. I was careful not to reveal too much, but I also didn't want to arouse suspicion.

As the conversation progressed, I noticed the investigator's eyes straying towards the desk. I knew I had to act fast.

"I'm afraid I have to get back to my duties," I said, rising from my chair. "But please, feel free to help yourself to more tea."

He nodded, his gaze returning to the bookshelves.

As I left the library, I felt a surge of adrenaline. I had bought Robert some time, but I knew it wouldn't be enough. The investigator was relentless, and he wouldn't rest until he had uncovered the truth.

I had to find a way to stop him. For my mother, for my own survival, and for the sake of the twisted justice I sought.

I retreated to the sanctuary of my room, to rest, as I closed my eyes, memories of my mother's hushed whispers flooding my mind. She had spoken of a man named Robert, a man whose charm masked a ruthless ambition and a capacity for cruelty. A man who had shattered her heart and left her to pick up the pieces of her shattered life.

The image of my mother, her face etched with pain and betrayal, fueled my determination to not relent. I had to know what Robert had done, what secrets he was so desperately trying to hide.

I began my search in the attic, a dusty repository of forgotten memories and discarded dreams. As I sifted through boxes of old photographs and yellowed letters, a picture began to emerge, a dark tapestry woven from threads of greed, deceit, and betrayal.

There were photographs of Robert with a woman who was not Katherine. Her name was Isabella, and she was the love of his life. But their love was doomed from the start, a forbidden romance that threatened to unravel the carefully constructed facade of the Bennett family.

Robert's father, a ruthless businessman in his own right, had arranged a marriage between Robert and Katherine, a union that would solidify the family's wealth and power. Isabella was cast aside, her dreams of a life with Robert shattered.

Broken and defeated, Isabella fled the country, leaving behind the only man she had ever loved. She disappeared into the shadows, her fate unknown.

As I pieced together the fragments of Isabella's story, a wave of anger washed over me. Robert had not only betrayed my mother, but he had also destroyed another woman's life. He was a monster, a predator who used his charm and power to manipulate and control those around him.

I vowed to make him pay for his sins, to expose his dark secrets and bring him to justice. But I knew it wouldn't be easy. Robert was a master manipulator, a cunning adversary who would stop at nothing to protect his empire.

The days following Detective Harrison's visit were fraught with a palpable tension. Robert, usually a picture of controlled composure, was on edge, his nerves frayed by the looming threat of exposure. Katherine retreated further into herself, a haunted look in her eyes as she contemplated the potential consequences of her husband's actions.

Unbeknownst to them, I was playing my own game, a dangerous dance of deception and manipulation. While feigning loyalty to the Bennetts, I subtly fed the investigator tidbits of information, carefully chosen morsels designed to pique his interest and lead him down the right path.

I watched as Detective Harrison delved deeper into the Bennetts' financial records, his meticulous investigation uncovering a labyrinth of shell companies, offshore accounts, and suspicious transactions. The deeper he dug, the more the rot of corruption revealed itself.

One afternoon, as I was dusting the study, I noticed a folder on Robert's desk labeled "Project Phoenix." Curiosity piqued, I glanced inside, my heart skipping a beat as I saw the incriminating documents within. It was a detailed plan outlining a scheme to defraud investors, a blatant act of corporate malfeasance that could bring down the entire Bennett empire.

I quickly replaced the folder, my mind racing with possibilities. This was it, the smoking gun that Detective Harrison needed. But how could I get it to him without arousing suspicion?

An opportunity presented itself that very evening. Robert had a business dinner, leaving Katherine and the children alone with me. After they had retired for the night, I crept into the study, my heart pounding in my chest. I retrieved the folder and made a copy of the documents, careful not to leave any trace of my intrusion.

The next morning, I slipped the copy into an envelope and addressed it to Detective Harrison. I then went about my daily routine, a sense of nervous anticipation thrumming through my veins.

Days turned into nights, and still, there was no word from the investigator. I began to doubt myself, to question whether I had made the right decision. Had I underestimated Robert's power and influence? Had I put myself in danger?

Then, one crisp morning, a police car pulled up in front of the Bennett mansion. Two officers emerged, their faces grim and determined. They approached the front door, their footsteps echoing through the silent house.

My heart leaped into my throat as I watched from the window. Had they come for Robert? Or had they discovered my involvement in the investigation? I braced myself for the confrontation, ready to face the consequences of my actions.

The doorbell rang, its shrill tone cutting through the tension. I took a deep breath, steeling myself for the inevitable. This was it, the moment of truth.

As I opened the door, I was met with the stern gaze of

Detective Harrison. He nodded curtly and stepped inside, his eyes scanning the room as if searching for clues.

"Evelyn," he said, his voice low and ominous. "We need to talk."

His words hung in the air, heavy with implication. A shiver ran down my spine, not from the autumnal chill seeping through the walls of the mansion, but from a deeper, more visceral fear. The investigator's presence had morphed from a mere obstacle into a looming threat, a danger not just to the Bennetts, but to my carefully constructed plans for retribution.

"Of course, Detective Harrison," I replied, my voice a careful blend of politeness and veiled apprehension. "Please, come in."

I stepped aside, allowing him to enter the foyer. He moved with a quiet confidence, his eyes scanning the surroundings like a predator assessing its prey. A wave of unease washed over me as I anticipate the full extent of the danger I was in.

He had uncovered the truth, or at least enough of it to pose a serious threat to my plans. The documents I had slipped him, the ones detailing Robert's illicit dealings, had clearly made an impact. But was that all he knew? Had he somehow connected me to the leak?

My mind raced, sifting through the possibilities, weighing the risks. Could I continue to play the innocent housemaid, or was it time to reveal my true identity and fight for my revenge head-on?

The investigator's gaze settled on me, his eyes narrowing as if he could see through my carefully crafted facade. "Evelyn," he began, his voice low and measured, "I have some questions for you about the Bennett family."

My heart hammered in my chest, but I maintained a calm exterior. "Of course, Detective. I'll answer to the best of my ability."

He studied me for a moment, a flicker of doubt crossing his face. Then, he nodded and gestured towards the living room. "Shall we?"

I led him into the opulent room, my mind racing as I tried to anticipate his questions. I knew I had to be careful, to choose my words wisely. One misstep could unravel everything.

As we sat down, the tension in the room thickened, a palpable force that pressed down on me like a physical weight. I could feel the investigator's eyes boring into me, his every movement radiating a quiet intensity.

"Evelyn," he began, his voice a gentle rumble, "I understand you've been working for the Bennetts for quite some time now."

I nodded, my throat tightening. "Yes, Detective. I've been with them for almost a year."

"And in that time," he continued, "you must have observed quite a bit."

His words hung in the air, heavy with unspoken accusations. I knew he was fishing for information, testing the waters to see how much I knew.

I took a deep breath, steeling myself for the battle that lay ahead. "I've seen my fair share, Detective," I replied, my voice carefully measured. "But I'm not one to gossip or spread rumors."

He raised an eyebrow, a hint of amusement in his eyes. "I'm not interested in gossip, Evelyn. I'm interested in the truth."

The truth. The word echoed in my mind, a stark reminder of the web of lies I had woven. I knew that I was walking a tightrope.

One wrong move, and I could fall into the abyss. I met his gaze with a carefully cultivated air of innocence. "I'm a simple housemaid, Detective," I said, my voice soft and demure. "I keep the house tidy, care for the children, and try to stay out of the family's affairs."

A wry smile played on his lips. "A simple housemaid with a keen eye for detail and a knack for being in the right place at the right time," he observed, his voice tinged with a hint of suspicion.

I felt a jolt of alarm. Was he onto me? Had he somehow figured out my true identity and my connection to the incriminating documents? I had to remain calm, to maintain the facade of ignorance I had so carefully crafted.

"I merely try to do my job to the best of my ability, Detective," I replied, feigning a look of confusion. "I don't understand what you're implying."

He leaned forward, his eyes fixed on mine. "Let's just say I have a feeling you know more than you're letting on, Evelyn," he said, his voice low and menacing.

A chill ran down my spine, but I refused to let him intimidate me. "With all due respect, Detective," I retorted, my voice firm and steady, "I'm not sure what you're hoping to gain by accusing me of something I have no knowledge of."

He sat back, a thoughtful expression on his face. "Perhaps you're right," he conceded, his tone softening slightly. "But I would be remiss if I didn't explore every avenue of investigation."

He paused, his gaze drifting towards the window. "Tell me, Evelyn," he said, his voice barely above a whisper, "what do you make of the Bennetts?"

I hesitated, unsure how to answer. I knew he was trying to trap me, to get me to reveal something that could incriminate myself.

"They're a complicated family," I finally replied, choosing my words carefully. "Like any family, I suppose. They have their fair share of dramas, their flaws. But they've always treated me with kindness and respect."

He nodded, seemingly satisfied with my answer. "And what about Robert Bennett?" he asked, his eyes narrowing. "What's your opinion of him?"

I felt a surge of anger, the memory of my mother's pain and suffering flooding back to me. But I quickly suppressed it, reminding myself that I couldn't afford to lose control.

"Mr. Bennett is a driven man," I said, my voice carefully neutral. "He's ambitious, determined, and fiercely protective of his family."

The investigator's lips curled into a sardonic smile. "Protective, you say?" he mused. "Or is it controlling?"

I shrugged, feigning indifference. "I wouldn't know, Detective. I merely observe what I see."

He studied me for a long moment, his eyes searching for any sign of deception. Then, he rose from his chair, his movements brisk and decisive.

"Thank you for your time, Evelyn," he said, his voice cold and formal. "I may have more questions for you later."

With that, he turned and left the room, leaving me alone with my thoughts. I exhaled slowly, the tension draining from my body. I had survived the encounter, but I knew it was just a temporary reprieve.

The investigator was a formidable opponent, a man driven by a thirst for justice and a keen intellect. I had to be smarter, faster, and more cunning if I wanted to outmaneuver him and achieve my revenge.

+++

CHAPTER 8

Unraveling Secrets

T he opulent facade of the Bennett family was crumbling, each crack widening with every passing day. Olivia, the once vibrant and promising daughter, had become a mere shadow of her former self, her life consumed by the insidious grip of addiction.

It started subtly, with a few missed appointments and a growing disinterest in her studies. But as the weeks turned into months, her decline became more pronounced. Her once radiant complexion grew sallow, her eyes dulled with a vacant stare, and her movements became sluggish and uncoordinated.

I watched her descent with a mixture of pity and satisfaction. I knew her addiction was a direct result of the immense pressure she felt to maintain the family's perfect image. The weight of their expectations had crushed her spirit, driving her to seek solace in the numbing embrace of drugs.

Her parents, blinded by their own ambition and denial, failed to recognize the depths of her despair. Robert, consumed by his corporate woes and the looming threat of the investigation, dismissed her erratic behavior as teenage rebellion. Katherine, lost in her own world of bitterness and resentment, turned a blind eye to her daughter's suffering.

One evening, as I was preparing dinner, I heard a commotion coming from the living room. I rushed in to find Olivia slumped on the couch, her body convulsing, her eyes rolled back in her head. A syringe lay discarded on the floor, a stark testament to her addiction.

Panic gripped me as I realized the severity of the situation. I shouted out to the whole house to call for an ambulance, my voice shaking with fear and desperation. As I waited for the paramedics to arrive, I held Olivia in my arms, whispering words of comfort and reassurance.

When the ambulance arrived, Olivia was rushed to the hospital, her life hanging in the balance. I followed in a taxi, my heart pounding in my chest. I knew that this incident would have far-reaching consequences for the Bennetts, but I couldn't help but feel a sense of responsibility for Olivia's well-being.

The news of Olivia's overdose spread like wildfire, a scandal that threatened to tarnish the Bennett family's pristine reputation. The media descended upon the hospital, their cameras flashing and their microphones thrust in my face as I emerged from the emergency room.

I fielded their questions with practiced ease, deflecting their inquiries with vague answers and carefully crafted statements. I knew I had to protect the family, to shield them from the prying eyes of the public. But I also couldn't ignore the growing sense of unease that gnawed at my conscience.

Olivia's downfall was a tragedy, a stark reminder of the destructive power of secrets and the corrosive nature of ambition. It was a wake-up call for the Bennetts, a stark reminder that their carefully constructed facade was crumbling, revealing the ugliness that lay beneath.

The Bennett name, once synonymous with success and prestige, was now splashed across the headlines for all the wrong reasons. The media, like vultures circling a dying carcass, descended upon the family, eager to feast on their misfortune.

The scandal surrounding Olivia's overdose had lifted the veil on the Bennetts' carefully curated image, exposing the cracks in their seemingly perfect facade. Reporters camped outside the mansion, their cameras flashing and their questions relentless.

"Mr. Bennett, can you comment on your daughter's addiction?"

"Mrs. Bennett, is it true that your family is facing financial ruin?"

"Evelyn, what can you tell us about the inner workings of the Bennett household?"

The constant scrutiny was taking its toll on Robert. He had always thrived on attention, on the adoration of the public. But now, the spotlight was harsh and unforgiving, revealing his flaws and vulnerabilities for all to see.

His business empire, already teetering on the brink of collapse due to the investigator's relentless pursuit, was now facing a new threat - the loss of investor confidence. The negative publicity surrounding Olivia's overdose had cast a shadow of doubt over the company's future, sending stock prices plummeting and sparking a wave of panic among shareholders.

Robert spent countless hours holed up in his study, his phone glued to his ear as he desperately tried to salvage the remnants of his empire. But his efforts were futile. The damage had been done, and the once mighty Bennett Corporation was crumbling under the weight of its own sins.

Katherine, meanwhile, retreated further into her own private hell. The shame and humiliation of her daughter's public downfall had shattered her already fragile spirit. She wandered through the mansion like a ghost, her eyes vacant and her movements mechanical.

Max, the silent observer, watched the chaos unfold with a mixture of sadness and anger. He blamed his parents for Olivia's addiction, for their neglect and their obsession with appearances. He felt abandoned, his childhood innocence shattered by the harsh realities of life.

Amidst the turmoil, I remained a silent observer, a chameleon blending into the background. But beneath my calm exterior, a storm raged. I knew that the Bennetts' downfall was imminent, and I was eager to witness their final reckoning.

The media frenzy, the crumbling empire, the shattered family - it was all I could wish for. I had played my part to set the wheels in motion, and now I was simply watching them spin out of control.

The air within the Bennett mansion crackled with a tension so thick it was almost palpable. The media circus outside had reached a fever pitch, the vultures of the press hungry for the next morsel of scandal. Inside, the silence was deafening, punctuated only by the rhythmic ticking of the grandfather clock and the occasional muffled sob from Katherine's room.

But the storm was brewing, and I knew it was only a matter of time before it unleashed its fury. Katherine, once a passive participant in her own life, had finally found her voice, fueled by a mother's anguish and a wife's betrayal.

One evening, as I was preparing dinner, I felt a presence behind me. I turned to find Katherine standing there, her eyes narrowed, her lips pressed into a thin line. Gone was the fragile, defeated woman I had grown accustomed to. In her place stood a warrior, ready to fight for her family, for her truth.

"We need to talk, Evelyn," she said, her voice low and steady.

I nodded, my heart pounding in my chest. The moment of confrontation had arrived. I followed her into the drawing-room, the setting sun casting long shadows that danced on the walls like grotesque figures.

Katherine gestured for me to sit, her movements deliberate and controlled. She then placed a small box on the table between us, her eyes never leaving mine.

"I found this in your room," she said, her voice barely above a whisper. "It seems you have a rather keen interest in my family's misfortunes."

I felt a surge of adrenaline, but I maintained my composure. "I'm not sure what you mean, Mrs. Bennett," I replied, my voice carefully neutral.

She opened the box, revealing the newspaper clippings and the photograph of my mother. "I think you know exactly what I mean, Evelyn," she said, her voice hardening. "Who are you, and what do you want from us?"

I took a deep breath, steeling myself for the inevitable. It was time to reveal my true identity, to lay my cards on the table.

"My name is not Evelyn," I began, my voice steady and resolute. "It's Anya."

A flicker of surprise crossed Katherine's face, but she quickly regained her composure. "Anya," she repeated, savouring the name. "A beautiful name. But it doesn't answer my question."

"I'm here for justice, Mrs. Bennett," I continued, my voice laced with a hint of bitterness. "For my mother, for myself, for all those who have suffered at the hands of your husband and your family."

Katherine's eyes widened, a mixture of shock and understanding dawning on her face. "You're Isabella's daughter," she whispered, her voice barely audible.

I nodded, my eyes fixed on hers. "Yes, Mrs. Bennett. I am."

A tense silence filled the room, the only sound the ticking of the grandfather clock. Then, Katherine leaned forward, her eyes blazing with a newfound determination.

"Tell me everything," she said, her voice firm and unwavering. "Tell me everything about your mother, about Robert, about what happened all those years ago."

I took a deep breath, ready to unleash the torrent of pain and anger that had been simmering within me for so long. The time for secrets was over. The time for truth had arrived.

The question hung heavy in the air, a silent accusation that echoed through the dimly lit room. I met Katherine's gaze head-on, my composure unwavering despite the turmoil raging within.

"My mother, Isabella," I began, my voice measured and deliberate, "was a kind and gentle woman, full of dreams and aspirations. She met your husband, Robert, when she was just a girl, and they fell deeply in love."

A flicker of pain crossed Katherine's face, a fleeting reminder of the love she had once shared with Robert. I pressed on, my words carefully chosen to elicit a specific reaction.

"But their love was forbidden," I continued, my voice laced with a hint of sorrow. "Robert's father, a ruthless businessman, forced him to marry you, a woman of his own social standing. Isabella.. my... my mother was heartbroken, cast out and treated like a slave. her life was shattered."

Katherine's eyes narrowed, her suspicion momentarily replaced by a flicker of sympathy. "I had no idea," she whispered, her voice barely audible.

I seized the opportunity to sow a seed of doubt. "Did you really not know, Mrs. Bennett?" I asked, my voice soft but pointed. "Or did you simply choose to look the other way?"

Katherine flinched, as if struck by a physical blow. "I... I didn't know," she stammered, her voice laced with guilt and shame.

I pressed on, my words like daggers piercing her fragile facade. "Your husband destroyed my mother's life," I said, my voice hardening. "He used her, manipulated her, and then discarded her like a broken toy. And you, Mrs. Bennett, were complicit in his cruelty."

Katherine's face paled, her eyes filled with a mixture of anger and despair. "No," she whispered, shaking her head vehemently. "No, I didn't know. I swear."

I watched her closely, gauging her reaction. Was she genuinely ignorant of her husband's past transgressions, or was she simply trying to protect herself from the truth?

"I find that hard to believe, Mrs. Bennett," I said, my voice dripping with skepticism. "You were married to the man for over two decades. Surely, you must have suspected or known something."

Katherine's composure finally cracked, tears streaming down her face. "I did," she sobbed, her voice thick with emotion. "I knew there was something wrong, but I was too afraid to confront him. I was afraid of what I might discover."

I rose from my chair and approached her, my voice softening as I spoke. "I understand your fear, Mrs. Bennett," I said, placing a comforting hand on her shoulder. "But the truth has a way of revealing itself, no matter how hard we try to bury it."

Katherine looked up at me, her eyes filled with a mixture of gratitude and desperation. "What are you going to do?" she asked, her voice trembling.

I smiled sadly, my heart heavy with the weight of my own secrets. "I'm going to get justice for my mother," I replied, my voice firm and resolute. "And I'm not going to let anyone, not even you, stand in my way."

With that, I turned and left the drawing-room, leaving Katherine to grapple with the painful truth of her husband's betrayal and her own complicity in his crimes.

The confrontation with Katherine left a bitter taste in my mouth, a chilling reminder of the destructive power of secrets and the heavy burden of revenge. As I sought solace in the solitude of my room, the shrill ring of the telephone shattered the silence.

My heart pounded in my chest when I remembered as I picked up the receiver, a sense of dread washing over me. It was the hospital, calling with news about my mother. Her condition had deteriorated significantly, her frail body succumbing to the ravages of her illness. The doctor's voice, grave and somber, informed me that she had mere days left, perhaps even hours.

A wave of grief and anger washed over me, threatening to drown me in its depths. My mother, the only person who had ever truly loved me, was slipping away, and I was powerless to stop it. I had devoted my life to avenging her suffering, to making the Bennetts pay for their sins. But now, time was running out, and I was torn between my desire for revenge and the growing affection I felt for Max.

He was an innocent caught in the crossfire, a victim of his parents' mistakes. I had grown fond of him, his inquisitive nature and gentle spirit a stark contrast to the toxic environment he was raised in. I couldn't bear the thought of hurting him, of inflicting pain on someone who had shown me nothing but kindness.

But I couldn't abandon my mission either. I had come too far, sacrificed too much. My mother's dying wish echoed in my ears, a constant reminder of the debt I owed her.

I paced my room, my mind racing as I tried to reconcile my conflicting emotions. The clock was ticking, and I had to make a decision. I couldn't let my affection for Max cloud my judgment, but I also couldn't ignore the moral implications of my actions.

I knew that my revenge would have consequences, that it would hurt not only the Bennetts but also those who were innocent bystanders. Max, Olivia, even Katherine, who had shown a glimmer of remorse for her husband's actions.

I had to find a way to balance my thirst for justice with my compassion for others. I had to find a way to honor my mother's memory without sacrificing my own humanity.

CHAPTER 9

The Dinner Party

The Bennett mansion was ablaze with light, a beacon of opulence against the darkening sky. As I flitted through the grand rooms, making final preparations for the dinner party, a sense of unease prickled at the back of my neck. This gathering was more than just a social affair; it was a carefully orchestrated performance, a desperate attempt by Robert to maintain the illusion of normalcy amidst the gathering storm.

Crystal chandeliers shimmered overhead, casting a warm glow on the polished marble floors. Exquisite floral arrangements, flown in from exotic locales, adorned every corner, their heady fragrance mingling with the subtle aroma of beeswax and lemon oil.

The dining table, a masterpiece of mahogany and mother-of-pearl, stretched the length of the room, its polished surface gleaming under the soft light of flickering candles. Each place setting was a work of art, a symphony of crystal, silver, and fine china. Gleaming cutlery, each piece bearing the Bennett family crest, lay perfectly aligned beside delicate porcelain plates.

The guest list was a veritable who's who of the city's elite: influential businessmen, renowned philanthropists, and socialites dripping with diamonds and designer gowns. Their laughter and chatter filled the air, a carefully constructed facade of gaiety that masked their underlying anxieties and unspoken secrets.

As the guests arrived, I moved amongst them, a silent

observer, a shadow blending into the background. I studied their faces, their body language, their subtle interactions. I listened to their conversations, gleaning valuable information, identifying potential allies and enemies.

The room buzzed with energy, a complex tapestry of ambition, envy, and hidden agendas. Each guest had their own reasons for attending this lavish affair, their own motivations for aligning themselves with the Bennett family.

The tension in the air was palpable, a simmering undercurrent of unease that threatened to erupt at any moment. I could feel the weight of expectation, the pressure to maintain the illusion of perfection.

But beneath the surface, I sensed a growing unease, a subtle shift in the balance of power. The cracks in the Bennett facade were widening, and the truth was slowly but surely seeping through.

The dinner party was a stage, a carefully constructed set designed to deceive and manipulate. But as the evening progressed, I knew that the masks would eventually fall, revealing the true faces of those who sought to profit from the Bennetts' downfall.

the Bennett family members moved like marionettes, their smiles strained, their movements robotic. A palpable tension simmered beneath the surface, threatening to shatter the illusion of normalcy they desperately clung to.

Robert, his face a mask of forced cheer, circulated among the guests, his booming laughter a stark contrast to the worry lines etched around his eyes. He shook hands, slapped backs, and exchanged pleasantries, all the while casting furtive glances towards Katherine, who sat at the head of the table, a brittle smile plastered on her face.

Katherine, once the epitome of grace and composure, now resembled a porcelain doll, her movements stiff and mechanical. Her eyes darted nervously around the room, as if searching for an escape route from the suffocating atmosphere of pretense.

Olivia, her gaunt face a testament to her recent ordeal, sat beside her mother, her gaze fixed on her plate. She picked at her food listlessly, her mind seemingly elsewhere. The shadow of her addiction lingered, a dark cloud that threatened to consume her entirely.

Max, the youngest of the Bennetts, was the only one who seemed oblivious to the underlying tension. His youthful innocence shielded him from the harsh realities of his family's situation. He chattered animatedly with the guest seated beside him, his laughter a brief respite from the oppressive atmosphere.

As the courses progressed, the tension at the table grew thicker. Forced smiles became more strained, polite conversation faltered, and awkward silences stretched uncomfortably long.

I moved among the guests, refilling glasses, clearing plates, and observing the subtle nuances of their interactions. I saw the pitying glances directed at Katherine, the whispers of speculation about Robert's business troubles, and the veiled contempt for Olivia's weakness.

The Bennetts, once the envy of society, were now the subject of gossip and ridicule. Their carefully constructed image had been shattered, and their fall from grace was a spectacle for all to see.

As the evening wore on, the tension reached a breaking point. A heated argument erupted between two of the guests, their voices rising above the din of polite conversation. Accusations were hurled, insults exchanged, and long-held grudges were aired.

The outburst was a catalyst, a spark that ignited the simmering resentment that had been brewing beneath the surface. The carefully orchestrated facade of civility crumbled, revealing the raw emotions that had been festering for so long.

The air thrummed with a discordant energy, the veneer of civility cracking under the strain of raw emotions. The dinner party had transformed into a battlefield, where words were weapons and social graces were discarded like tattered shields. I, however, remained a tranquil eye in the storm, a silent observer amidst the chaos.

Moving through the fragmented conversations, I became an unseen conductor, subtly orchestrating a symphony of revelations. With a well-placed question here, a seemingly innocent comment there, I steered discussions toward the family's vulnerabilities, nudging the guests towards the precipice of truth.

I paused beside a group of businessmen huddled in a corner, their voices lowered in hushed whispers. "Such a shame about the recent downturn in Bennett Corp's stock," I remarked, my voice a delicate blend of concern and curiosity. "I do hope Mr. Bennett can weather the storm."

Their eyes widened, a flicker of interest sparking in their

depths. The conversation shifted, whispers turning into open speculation about Robert's financial woes, his questionable business practices, and the impending investigation.

Next, I found myself in the company of a group of socialites, their painted smiles masking their predatory instincts. "Poor Olivia," I sighed, my voice laden with sympathy. "Addiction is such a terrible disease. I can't imagine what her family must be going through."

Their eyes lit up, gossip-hungry mouths watering at the prospect of scandal. They leaned in, eager to share their own theories about Olivia's downfall, her parents' supposed neglect, and the scandalous rumors swirling around the Bennett name.

As the night wore on, the conversations grew more heated, fueled by alcohol and a growing sense of moral superiority. Secrets were whispered, accusations were hurled, and the Bennetts' carefully constructed facade crumbled further with each passing moment.

I moved among the guests, a phantom in the shadows, feeding their curiosity, stoking their resentment, and fanning the flames of their animosity. I was a master puppeteer, pulling the strings of their emotions, manipulating them to my own ends.

With each revelation, with each whispered accusation, the Bennetts' world grew darker, their secrets laid bare for all to see. And I, the silent observer, the unseen conductor, reveled in their downfall, knowing that my time for vengeance was drawing near.

The dinner party was a turning point, a pivotal moment in my quest for justice. I had exposed the Bennetts' vulnerabilities, their weaknesses, and their deepest fears. I had laid the groundwork for their destruction, and I was ready to deliver the final blow.

I glided through the opulent room, a silent predator in a sea of unsuspecting prey. The escalating tension and the rising decibel of voices provided the perfect cover for my machinations. I sought out Robert, who stood isolated in a corner, nursing a tumbler of whiskey and wearing a mask of forced joviality. His eyes darted around the room, a mixture of arrogance and anxiety battling for dominance.

"Mr. Bennett," I began, my voice laced with concern, "you seem troubled. Is everything alright?"

He looked at me, startled for a moment, then a wry smile twisted his lips. "Troubled? Me? Never, Evelyn. Just a few minor setbacks, nothing I can't handle."

I tilted my head, feigning sympathy. "I'm so sorry to hear that, sir. But you're a strong man, Mr. Bennett. I'm sure you'll overcome any obstacle."

My words, a carefully crafted blend of empathy and subtle flattery, hit their mark. Robert straightened his shoulders, his ego momentarily soothed by my admiration.

"Of course, Evelyn," he boasted, his voice rising slightly. "I've built an empire from nothing. A few setbacks won't deter me."

I nodded, my eyes wide with admiration. "You're an inspiration, Mr. Bennett," I gushed. "A true visionary."

He puffed up his chest, his arrogance growing with each word of praise. "You're too kind, Evelyn," he said, a smug grin spreading across his face. "But it's true. I've always been a step ahead of the competition. I see opportunities where others see obstacles."

I leaned in, lowering my voice to a conspiratorial whisper. "I'm sure that's why you're not worried about this investigation," I said, my eyes fixed on his. "You've got everything under control."

A flicker of doubt crossed his face, a fleeting moment of vulnerability. But it was quickly replaced by a mask of bravado.

"The investigation is a minor inconvenience," he scoffed, waving his hand dismissively. "A nuisance, nothing more. Those bureaucrats don't understand the complexities of high finance. They're chasing shadows, barking up the wrong tree."

I nodded, feigning agreement. "I'm sure you're right, Mr. Bennett," I said, my voice dripping with sycophantic admiration. "You're always one step ahead."

My words, like honeyed poison, fueled his ego, lulling him into a false sense of security. He relaxed, his guard lowered, his tongue loosened by the intoxicating blend of alcohol and flattery.

As the conversation continued, Robert grew more animated, his words becoming increasingly reckless and unguarded. He boasted about his business dealings, his political connections, and his ability to manipulate the system.

I listened intently, absorbing every detail, every nuance. I was a sponge, soaking up information that would prove invaluable in my quest for revenge.

Robert, blinded by his own hubris, revealed more than he intended. He spoke of offshore accounts, and shady transactions, and even hinted at illegal activities. He was digging his own grave, and I was the silent gravedigger, eagerly awaiting the moment to shovel the first mound of dirt.

As the night wore on, Robert's words became increasingly slurred, his composure dissolving into a drunken stupor. I watched him with a mixture of disgust and satisfaction. He was a pathetic figure, a shadow of the man he once was.

I knew that I had won. I had successfully manipulated him, extracted the information I needed, and exposed his true nature. The dinner party, a desperate attempt to maintain the illusion of control, had backfired spectacularly.

In the aftermath of the chaotic dinner party, the Bennett

mansion was shrouded in a tense silence. The echoes of raised voices and shattered illusions still lingered in the air, a constant reminder of the family's unraveling. As I navigated the debris of the evening, clearing away the remnants of the feast, my mind raced with the implications of Robert's reckless revelations. The investigator now had enough ammunition to bring down the Bennett empire, and my revenge seemed within reach.

Yet, a nagging unease gnawed at me. My growing affection for Max had become a thorn in my side, a constant reminder of the innocence that I was in danger of corrupting. His unwavering trust in me, despite the turmoil swirling around him, was a heavy burden to bear.

One morning, as I was helping Max with his homework in the library, he looked up at me with a troubled expression. "Evelyn," he began hesitantly, "I need to tell you something."

My heart skipped a beat. Had has he discovered? Did he know about my plans for revenge?

"What is it, Max?" I asked, my voice barely above a whisper.

He hesitated, his eyes darting around the room as if searching for the right words. "I... I found something in your room," he confessed, his voice barely audible.

"What did you find, Max?" I asked, trying to keep my voice steady.

He took a deep breath, his eyes meeting mine with a newfound determination. "I found a box," he said, his voice gaining strength, "with newspaper articles about my family, and a picture of a woman. I think... I think she's your mother."

A wave of relief washed over me. He had found the box, but he hadn't connected the dots. He still saw me as Evelyn, the kind and caring housemaid, not the vengeful daughter seeking retribution.

"Yes, Max," I confirmed, my voice soft and reassuring. "That was my mother. She passed away a few years ago."

A look of sadness crossed his face, and he reached out to take my hand. "I'm sorry, Evelyn," he said, his voice thick with emotion. "I didn't mean to pry."

I squeezed his hand gently. "It's alright, Max," I reassured him. "I understand your curiosity."

He looked at me for a long moment, his eyes filled with a mixture of trust and confusion. Then, he spoke again, his voice barely above a whisper. "I think you're the only one who truly cares about me, Evelyn," he said, his words piercing my heart like a dagger.

I felt a surge of conflicting emotions. I wanted to hug him, to comfort him, to tell him the truth. But I knew I couldn't. I had a mission to complete, a promise to fulfill.

"I care about you too, Max," I whispered, my voice choked with emotion. "More than you know."

He smiled, a faint glimmer of hope in his eyes. But then, he hesitated, as if a thought had just occurred to him.

"Evelyn," he began, his voice barely audible, "I think I should tell my mother about the box I found."

My heart stopped. If Max told Katherine about the box, it would be game over. My carefully crafted facade would shatter, and my revenge would be thwarted.

I had to stop him.

"Max," I began, my voice a gentle caress, "your mother is going through a very difficult time right now. The stress of Olivia's situation has taken a toll on her, and I don't want to burden her with anything else."

He looked at me, his eyes filled with concern. "But Evelyn," he protested, "this is important. I think she needs to know."

I knelt down beside him, taking his hands in mine. "I know it seems important to you, Max," I said, my voice soft and reassuring. "But trust me, it's not the right time. Your mother needs our support, not more worries."

He hesitated, his brow furrowed in thought. I could see the conflict raging within him, the battle between his desire to do the right thing and his concern for his mother's well-being.

"But... what about the woman in the picture?" he asked, his voice barely a whisper. "Who was she?"

I took a deep breath, summoning all my composure. "That was my mother," I explained, my voice filled with a carefully crafted sorrow. "She was a kind and gentle woman, and she loved your family very much. She kept those newspaper clippings as a way of staying connected to them, of feeling like she was a part of their lives."

Max's eyes widened with surprise. "She loved my family?" he asked, his voice tinged with disbelief.

I nodded, a single tear rolling down my cheek. "Yes, Max," I confirmed, my voice thick with emotion. "She admired your parents, their success, their generosity. She dreamed that one day, you and I would have the opportunity to experience their world, to be a part of something special."

Max's expression softened, his suspicion replaced by a look of understanding and empathy. "I see," he said quietly. "So, those clippings weren't... weren't about anything bad?"

I shook my head, my voice barely above a whisper. "No, Max. They were a testament to my mother's love for your family."

He seemed to accept my explanation, his eyes filled with a newfound trust. He reached out and hugged me tightly, his small arms wrapped around my neck.

"Thank you, Evelyn," he whispered, his voice muffled against my shoulder. "I'm glad you told me."

I hugged him back, my heart heavy with the weight of my deception. I had averted a crisis, but I knew that this was just a temporary reprieve. Max's curiosity had been piqued, and I would have to tread even more carefully in the future.

As I watched him leave the library, a sense of unease settled over me. I had narrowly escaped, but I knew that the investigator was closing in. The net was tightening, and I had to act quickly if I wanted to achieve my revenge before it was too late.

I took a deep breath, the weight of my secrets pressing down on me like a physical burden. Max's innocent gaze, filled with a mixture of trust and hope, was a mirror reflecting my own conflicted soul.

The revelation of Robert's past misdeeds had shattered any remaining illusions of happiness, leaving Katherine teetering on the precipice of despair.

She had spent years burying her suspicions, her fears, and her own desires beneath layers of societal expectations and wifely duty. But now, the truth had been unearthed, and she could no longer deny the toxic reality of her marriage.

The confrontation came on a stormy night, the wind howling outside like a banshee heralding the impending doom. Robert, fueled by a potent mixture of anger and alcohol, stumbled into the bedroom, his face contorted in a mask of fury.

"Where were you?" he snarled, his voice slurring slightly. "I've been looking all over for you."

Katherine, her resolve hardened by the revelations of the past few days, stood tall, her eyes blazing with defiance. "I was speaking with Ellen," she replied, her voice calm and steady.

Robert's eyes narrowed, his suspicion piqued. " Ellen?" he questioned, his voice laced with venom. "What were you talking about with Ellen?"

"We were talking about you, Robert," Katherine retorted, her voice rising with each word. "We were talking about your lies, your deceit, and your betrayal."

Robert's face paled, his bravado momentarily faltering. "What are you talking about?" he stammered, his voice barely above a whisper.

"I know everything, Robert," Katherine declared, her voice ringing with newfound power. Robert's composure crumbled. "I was foolish., it was a mistake, It didn't mean anything," his voice weak and pathetic.

Katherine laughed bitterly, her eyes filled with contempt. "It didn't mean anything?" she repeated, her voice dripping with sarcasm. "You destroyed a woman's life, Robert. You broke her heart, ruined her reputation, and left her with nothing."

"It was a mistake," Robert insisted, his voice laced with desperation. "I regret it every day of my life."

"Regret?" Katherine scoffed. "Is that one of the many secrets you've been hiding from me? Is that... you've been lying ..., cheating on me...hhh?"

Robert recoiled as if struck, his face contorted in a mask of shame and anger. "You have no right to judge me," he spat, his voice laced with venom. "You knew what you were getting into when you married me. You knew I was ambitious, ruthless, and willing to do whatever it took to succeed."

"Yes, I knew," Katherine admitted, her voice barely a whisper. "But I didn't know you were a monster."

Robert lunged towards her, his hands outstretched, but she quickly stepped back, her eyes blazing with defiance. "Don't touch me," she warned, her voice cold and sharp. "I'm done with you, Robert. I'm done with this life."

She turned and walked towards the door, her movements swift and decisive. "I'm leaving you," she declared, her voice echoing through the room. "I'm taking the children."

Robert stood frozen in one place, his face a mask of shock and disbelief. He had lost everything, his wife, his family, his reputation. The empire he had built on a foundation of lies and deceit was crumbling around him, and he was powerless to stop it.

Katherine's words hung in the air, a silent indictment of Robert's character and their crumbling marriage. The once opulent bedroom, a sanctuary of shared dreams and whispered secrets, now felt like a battleground.

Robert, fueled by rage and wounded pride, lashed out, his voice a venomous hiss. "You ungrateful witch!" he spat, his face contorted in a grotesque mask of fury. "After everything I've given you, this is how you repay me?"

He lunged towards Katherine, his hands outstretched, but she nimbly sidestepped his clumsy advance. "Don't touch me!" she shrieked, her voice laced with disgust. "You disgust me."

Robert stumbled, his eyes wild with rage. "You're nothing without me!" he roared, his voice echoing through the room. "You're a nobody, a social climber who latched onto my name and my money. You wouldn't survive a day without me!"

Katherine's eyes flashed with defiance. "Don't you dare underestimate me, Robert," she retorted, her voice icy cold. "I may have been blind to your lies and your deceit, but I'm not stupid.

Robert's face paled, his bravado replaced by a look of panic. "You wouldn't dare," he threatened, his voice barely above a whisper. "You'll lose everything. The house, the cars, the lifestyle you've grown so accustomed to. You'll be nothing without me."

Katherine laughed bitterly, her eyes filled with contempt. "I'd rather be nothing than continue to live with a monster like you," she spat, her words piercing his fragile ego like a dagger.

The fight escalated, their voices rising and falling in a symphony of accusation and recrimination. Robert, fueled by a lifetime of entitlement and arrogance, refused to accept defeat. He hurled insults, threatened to ruin her, to take away everything she held dear.

Katherine, however, stood her ground, her resolve strengthened by the knowledge of his betrayal. She threw his own words back at him, exposing his hypocrisy and cruelty.

The bedroom became a war zone, a battleground of shattered dreams and broken promises. Furniture was overturned, vases smashed, and the air throbbed with the intensity of their emotions.

Unseen, Max peered through the cracked doorway, his small frame trembling as he witnessed the brutal dismantling of his family. His eyes were wide with fear and confusion, his heart aching with the pain of betrayal.

The illusion of a happy family, once a comforting shield against the harsh realities of the world, was now shattered beyond repair. The cracks had widened into gaping wounds, exposing the festering rot that had been hidden beneath the surface for so long.

Max watched in horror as his parents tore each other apart, their love replaced by a toxic cocktail of anger, resentment, and loathing. He wanted to scream, to run away, to escape the nightmare that was unfolding before his eyes.

But he couldn't move, couldn't speak, couldn't even breathe. He was frozen in place, a silent witness to the destruction of his family.

The echoes of the shattering fight reverberated through the house, each slammed door, each raised voice, a jarring note in the symphony of destruction. The once grand Bennett mansion now felt like a hollow shell, its walls echoing with the ghosts of a shattered family.

From the shadows of the hallway, unseen and unheard, I witnessed the implosion of the Bennett family. The veneer of civility had been ripped away, revealing the raw wounds of betrayal, resentment, and despair that festered beneath the surface.

Katherine's revelation of Robert's past misdeeds had struck a chord deep within me. The pain in her voice, the raw anguish etched on her face, mirrored the suffering my mother had endured. In that moment, I saw Katherine not as the enemy, but as a fellow victim, a woman trapped in a gilded cage of her own making.

The sight of Max, his small frame trembling with fear and confusion, tugged at my heartstrings. His innocence, his unwavering trust in me, had chipped away at the hardened shell I had built around myself. I saw in him a reflection of my own childhood, a time when I believed in the inherent goodness of people before the harsh realities of life shattered my illusions.

A deep conflict raged within me, a battle between my thirst for vengeance and the burgeoning empathy I felt for the Bennetts. My carefully constructed plan for revenge seemed hollow, and meaningless in the face of their pain and suffering.

Was this truly justice? To inflict pain on a family already teetering on the brink of collapse? To shatter the lives of innocent children caught in the crossfire of their parents' war?

The questions haunted me, their answers elusive and unsettling. I had spent years nurturing my anger, feeding the flames of hatred that consumed me. But now, faced with the raw emotions of the Bennetts, I questioned the righteousness of my path.

I thought of Max, his innocent eyes filled with trust and hope. Could I betray that trust? Could I break his heart by exposing his father's crimes?

The image of my mother, her face etched with pain and betrayal, flashed before my eyes. Her dying wish, her plea for justice, echoed in my ears. Could I betray her memory by abandoning my quest for revenge?

I was trapped in a moral dilemma, torn between my desire for vengeance and my growing empathy for the Bennetts. The path ahead was unclear, shrouded in doubt and uncertainty.

I knew that I had to make a choice, a choice that would determine not only the fate of the Bennetts but also my destiny. But which path would I choose? The path of revenge, fueled by anger and hatred? Or the path of compassion, guided by empathy and forgiveness?

The answer, I realized, lay not in the past, but in the present. It lay in the eyes of a young boy who had shown me kindness and trust, in the heart of a woman who had been wronged and betrayed.

I had to find a way to reconcile my conflicting emotions, to find a balance between justice and mercy. I had to find a way to honor my mother's memory without sacrificing my humanity.

CHAPTER 11

The Truth Emerges

The investigator's relentless pursuit, the mounting evidence of his misdeeds, and Katherine's shocking revelations had chipped away at his carefully constructed facade, exposing the rot that festered beneath the surface.

In a desperate attempt to regain control, he sought me out, his eyes bloodshot and his voice thick with barely suppressed rage. "Evelyn," he barked, his tone a stark contrast to the false charm he usually exuded, "I need to speak with you."

A cold knot tightened in my stomach as I walked towards Robert's study. His summons had been unexpected, his tone chillingly calm. It was a tone that suggested he knew. My mind raced, replaying every interaction, every carefully crafted word and gesture. Had I slipped up? Revealed a hint of my true intentions?

As I entered the dimly lit study, Robert stood by the window, his back to me. He turned slowly, his eyes boring into mine with an intensity that sent shivers down my spine. "Evelyn," he began, his voice low and measured, "we need to talk."

My heart pounded in my chest, but I maintained a facade of composure. "Of course, Mr. Bennett. What is it?"

He took a step closer, the air crackling with unspoken tension. "I know who you are," he said, his voice barely above a whisper. "I know why you're here."

The words hung heavy in the air, suffocating me. I felt a cold sweat break out on my skin. Had he discovered my secret? Was my carefully constructed plan about to crumble before my eyes?

I met his gaze, refusing to back down. "I don't understand what you mean, Mr. Bennett," I said, my voice trembling slightly. "I'm just the housemaid."

He let out a humorless laugh. "Don't play games with me, Evelyn," he said. "I know about your mother. I know about her...relationship with me."

A wave of nausea washed over me. So he knew. The truth I had so carefully buried had been unearthed. My mind raced, trying to formulate a response, but the words caught in my throat.

Robert continued, his voice laced with a mixture of anger and sadness. "I did her wrong, Evelyn. I admit that. But what you're doing...it's not the answer. It's not justice."

I clenched my fists, fighting back tears. "Justice?" I spat out the word like a curse. "what do you call what you did to my mother? You left her with nothing, Robert. You destroyed her life."

He sighed, running a hand through his hair. "I was young and foolish," he said. "I made mistakes. But that doesn't justify what you're doing."

I took a step closer, my voice rising. "You think this is about revenge, Robert? It's not. It's about setting things right. It's about making you pay for what you did."

His eyes narrowed. "And what about the children, Evelyn? What about Katherine? They're innocent in all of this."

Guilt gnawed at me. I hadn't considered the collateral damage. My focus had been solely on Robert, on making him suffer as my mother had suffered. But what about the others? Were they to be casualties in my quest for vengeance?

I hesitated, my resolve wavering. Perhaps Robert was right. Perhaps this path was not the answer. But as I looked into his eyes, I saw a flicker of fear, of desperation. And I knew that I couldn't back down now. I had come too far.

"They'll be fine, Robert," I said, my voice hardening. "They'll survive. But you...you won't."

A chilling silence descended upon the room. The air crackled with unspoken threats and simmering resentment. We stood there, locked in a silent battle of wills, each knowing that the other was the enemy.

Robert's face paled, his bravado momentarily replaced by a flicker of fear. A bitter satisfaction surged through me, but it was short-lived. A sudden noise from behind the half-closed door leading to the conservatory startled me.

I held my breath, straining to hear. A muffled gasp followed by the distinct sound of retreating footsteps. Someone had been listening. Panic clawed at me. Who could it be?

Before I could react, the door creaked open, revealing a figure I hadn't expected – Katherine. Her eyes were wide with shock, her face pale. My heart sank. Of all people, why did it have to be her?

Katherine's gaze darted between Robert and me, her lips trembling as she struggled to speak. "What... what's going on here?" she finally managed, her voice barely a whisper.

I glanced at Robert, who looked equally stunned. The truth had been revealed, not in the way I had planned, but it was out in the open nonetheless. I felt a strange mix of emotions – triumph, guilt, and a growing sense of dread.

Katherine's initial shock quickly gave way to a fierce determination. Her eyes hardened as she took a step towards me, her voice filled with a protective fury I hadn't anticipated. "You," she spat, pointing a trembling finger at me. "You're not who you say you are. You've been lying to us all along."

I opened my mouth to respond, but no words came out. What

could I say? That she was right? That I had infiltrated her home with the sole purpose of destroying her husband? The weight of my deception pressed down on me, threatening to crush me.

Katherine turned to Robert, her voice filled with accusation. "And you," she said, her voice shaking with rage. "You knew about this? You brought this...this viper into our home?"

Robert opened his mouth to speak, but Katherine cut him off. "Don't you dare defend her," she hissed. "You've done enough damage already."

Her words were like a slap in the face. The anger in her eyes was palpable, but beneath it, I saw something else – fear. Fear for her children, for their safety.

A wave of guilt washed over me. I had been so consumed by my pain, my thirst for revenge, that I hadn't considered the impact my actions would have on others. I had underestimated Katherine, her strength, her love for her family.

As I watched her protectively gather her children, ushering them away from the unfolding drama, I knew that my carefully laid plans were about to unravel. The game had changed, and the stakes were higher than ever before.

The air thrummed with tension, each breath a taut wire stretched to its limit. Katherine's presence had cast an unexpected shadow over the battlefield of our confrontation. Her maternal instincts had overridden her shock, her love for her children a shield against the storm brewing between Robert and me.

Her voice, though trembling, was resolute as she addressed us. "Enough!" she commanded, stepping between us with a surprising forcefulness. "This madness ends now."

Her gaze swept from Robert's ashen face to mine, her eyes filled with a mixture of anger and pleading. "Evelyn," she began, her voice softening slightly, "I don't know what has happened between you and Robert, but this... this isn't the way. Think of the children."

Her words struck a chord within me, a pang of guilt piercing through my carefully constructed armor of vengeance. I had been so consumed by my own pain that I hadn't truly considered the innocent lives that would be caught in the crossfire. Olivia, with her fragile spirit, and Max, with his innocent curiosity – they didn't deserve to be dragged into this.

Katherine turned to Robert, her voice laced with disappointment and reproach. "And you," she said, her voice shaking with barely restrained anger, "you have a lot to answer for. But this isn't the time or place."

Her gaze returned to me, her eyes pleading for understanding. "Evelyn," she said, her voice barely a whisper, "please. There has to be another way."

I looked at her, at the woman I had grown to respect and admire, despite my sinister intentions. I saw the pain in her eyes, and the fear for her children's well-being. It was a reflection of the pain I had carried for so long, the pain Robert had inflicted on my mother.

But something shifted within me. A flicker of doubt, a glimmer of humanity that I had thought long extinguished. Could there be another way? A way to achieve justice without causing further harm?

I opened my mouth to speak, but the words caught in my throat. The weight of my past, of my mother's suffering, pressed down on me, suffocating any possibility of reconciliation. Yet, a part of me, a small, hopeful part, yearned to believe that there could be a different path, a path that didn't end in destruction.

The silence stretched on, each second a torturous eternity. Robert and I remained locked in a tense standoff, the air thick with unspoken animosity. Katherine's intervention had created a momentary pause, a chance for reason to prevail. But would it be enough to quell the storm that had been brewing for so long?

Katherine's voice, soft yet unwavering, broke through the suffocating tension. "Evelyn," she pleaded, her gaze locking onto mine, "think of Olivia. Think of Max. They love you. They trust you."

Her words again struck a nerve, a raw and exposed vulnerability I had tried so desperately to bury. The image of Olivia's wide-eyed innocence and Max's eager smile flashed before me, a painful reminder of the collateral damage I had been willing to inflict.

"They don't deserve to be hurt," Katherine continued, her voice trembling slightly. "They shouldn't have to bear the burden of our past mistakes."

My chest tightened, a suffocating guilt rising within me. I had been so consumed by my thirst for revenge, that I had blinded myself to the innocent lives that would be caught in the crossfire. Olivia, with her fragile spirit and budding dreams, and Max, with his infectious laughter and unwavering trust – they were not pawns in my game.

"I know you've been hurt, Evelyn," Katherine said, her voice softening. "I can see the pain in your eyes. But hurting others won't heal your wounds. It will only create more pain, more suffering."

Her words resonated within me, echoing the whispers of my conscience that I had tried so desperately to ignore. I had convinced myself that my actions were justified, that revenge was the only way to right the wrongs of the past. But as I looked at Katherine, at the genuine concern etched on her face, I realized that I had been wrong.

"There has to be another way," Katherine pleaded, her voice filled with desperation. "A way to find peace, to find justice, without destroying everything in your path."

I wanted to believe her, to believe that there was a way to escape the cycle of pain and vengeance that had consumed my life. But the doubts lingered, the scars of the past too deep to be easily erased.

A thick silence descended upon the room, broken only by the ragged breaths of the three of us. The air crackled with unspoken accusations, each of us locked in our private torment. Katherine's unexpected intervention had momentarily halted the momentum of our confrontation, leaving us suspended in a precarious balance.

Robert, his face a mask of conflicting emotions, finally broke the silence. "Katherine, my love," he began, his voice strained, "this isn't what it looks like."

His words dripped with insincerity, a desperate attempt to regain control of a situation that was rapidly spiraling out of his grasp. But Katherine wasn't swayed. Her eyes, once filled with love and admiration, now held a steely resolve.

"Don't insult my intelligence, Robert," she retorted, her voice cold and sharp. "I heard enough to know that you've been keeping secrets from me. Secrets that could destroy our family."

Her words were like a dagger, piercing through Robert's carefully constructed facade. He flinched as if struck, his composure crumbling under the weight of her accusation.

I watched the exchange with a mixture of satisfaction and unease. Part of me reveled in Robert's discomfort, in the unraveling of his carefully crafted image. But another part of me, the part that Katherine had awakened, felt a growing sense of unease. This wasn't how I had envisioned things.

The tension in the room escalated, the air thick with unspoken threats and simmering resentment. Robert's eyes darted between Katherine and me, his desperation growing with each passing second.

Suddenly, he lunged towards me, his hands outstretched, his face contorted with rage. "You bitch!" he snarled, his voice raw with fury. "You've ruined everything!"

I instinctively recoiled, but his fingers grazed my arm, sending a jolt of fear through me. Katherine screamed, her voice piercing the tense silence. She threw herself between us, her body a fragile barrier against Robert's wrath.

"Stop it!" she cried, her voice filled with a desperate urgency. "Both of you!"

But Robert was beyond reason. He shoved Katherine aside, his eyes fixed on me with a murderous intensity. I knew in that moment that he would stop at nothing to protect his secrets, to silence me forever.

A surge of adrenaline coursed through my veins. I was not the helpless victim I had once been. I had learned to fight, to defend myself. As Robert lunged again, I sidestepped, my movements swift and practiced.

The room erupted into chaos, a whirlwind of flailing limbs and guttural cries. Furniture toppled, glass shattered, the once pristine study transformed into a battleground. In the midst of the struggle, I caught a glimpse of Katherine, her eyes wide with terror as she tried to intervene.

But it was too late. The forces we had unleashed were beyond our control, spiraling towards a devastating conclusion

The room became a whirlwind of desperation and fury. Robert, fueled by a cocktail of panic and rage, was like a cornered animal, lashing out blindly. I twisted and turned, narrowly dodging his wild swings, my heart pounding in my chest. Each near miss fueled my adrenaline, sharpening my reflexes, and heightening my senses.

But Katherine, caught in the crossfire, wasn't as agile. In a desperate attempt to intervene, she lunged forward, her arms outstretched as if to shield me from Robert's wrath. But her noble gesture was met with a cruel twist of fate.

As Robert and I struggled, my elbow connected with Katherine's chest, sending her stumbling backward. A sickening thud echoed through the room as her head collided with the sharp edge of the mahogany desk. Time seemed to slow to a crawl as she crumpled to the floor, a crimson stain blossoming on the pristine carpet.

The world went silent. The only sound was the erratic thud of my own heartbeat. A wave of nausea washed over me as I stared at Katherine's motionless form. A million thoughts raced through my mind, each more horrifying than the last.

Robert, his face drained of color, stood frozen, his hands still outstretched as if suspended in mid-air. The rage that had consumed him moments before had vanished, replaced by a look of utter disbelief and horror.

I knelt beside Katherine, my hands trembling as I reached for her pulse. It was faint, barely there. A warm stickiness coated my fingers as I gently lifted her head. A gash on her temple oozed blood, staining her pale skin.

A strangled sob escaped my lips as the full weight of the situation crashed down upon me. I had never intended for anyone to get hurt, least of all Katherine. She was innocent, a victim of my misguided quest for revenge.

Panic surged through me, blurring my vision and clouding my thoughts. I looked up at Robert, pleading for him to do something, to take control of the situation. But he just stood there, his eyes wide with shock, his body paralyzed by fear.

In that moment, I realized the horrifying truth. We were alone. Alone with a dying woman, the blood staining our hands, the guilt suffocating our souls.

Time seemed to fracture, the seconds stretching into an eternity of agonizing silence. The only sound in the room was the rhythmic drip of Katherine's blood, each drop a stark reminder of the tragedy that had unfolded.

I remained kneeling beside her, my hands hovering over her wound, useless in the face of the damage I had caused. A wave of nausea washed over me, threatening to overwhelm my senses. My stomach churned, and I could feel bile rising in my throat.

Robert finally snapped out of his stupor, his eyes darting frantically between Katherine and me. "We have to call an ambulance," he said, his voice barely a whisper.

"It's too late," I choked out, my voice thick with despair. "She's... she's gone."

Denial flashed across Robert's face, a desperate attempt to cling to a shred of hope. "No," he insisted, shaking his head. "No, no, no..."

He knelt beside me, his hands trembling as he reached for Katherine's wrist. After a moment, he slumped back, his shoulders sagging in defeat. "She's gone," he echoed, his voice hollow.

A sob escaped my lips, and I buried my face in my hands, the sobs wracking my body. The guilt was overwhelming, a suffocating weight that threatened to crush me. I had never intended for this to happen. I had never wanted to hurt anyone, least of all Katherine.

Robert remained silent, his gaze fixed on Katherine's lifeless body. The anger and fear that had consumed him moments before had vanished, replaced by a deep sadness and a profound sense of loss.

As the initial shock wore off, I felt a burning rage ignite within me. This wasn't supposed to happen. My plan had been to expose Robert's crimes, to make him pay for what he had done to my mother. But now, an innocent life had been lost, a family shattered.

I looked at Robert, my eyes blazing with fury. "This is your fault," I spat out, my voice filled with venom. "You brought this upon us. You and your lies, your deceit."

He didn't respond, his gaze still fixed on Katherine. The silence stretched on, thick with unspoken accusations and recriminations.

In that moment, I realized the devastating truth. My quest for revenge had spiraled out of control, leaving a trail of destruction in its wake. I had become the very thing I had sought to destroy.

CHAPTER 12

Fallout

Robert's initial gasp of horror gradually morphed into a different kind of panic. The blood drained from his face, not just from the shock of Katherine's injury but also from the cold dread seeping into his eyes. It was the look of a man who had built a life on carefully constructed lies, now terrified of the impending collapse.

His gaze darted around the room, taking in the overturned furniture, the shattered vase, and finally settling on Katherine's still form. His voice, when it finally came, was barely a croak. "We... we have to do something."

I looked up at him, my own mind racing, my emotions a tangled mess of guilt and fear. "We have to call for help," I choked out, the words barely audible.

But Robert shook his head, his eyes wide with a desperate urgency. "No," he said, his voice barely a whisper. "No hospitals, no police. They'll ask questions. They'll find out..."

His voice trailed off, but the unspoken implication hung heavy in the air. He was worried about himself, about being implicated in Katherine's death. The self-preservation instinct, so deeply ingrained in his nature, had kicked in, overriding any concern he might have had for his wife.

A surge of disgust and anger rose within me. How could he be so callous? So focused on protecting himself when his wife lay bleeding on the floor and lifeless?

"We can't just leave her here!" I cried, my voice rising in

desperation. "She needs help!"

But Robert was already shaking his head, his resolve hardening. "We have to make this look like an accident," he said, his voice cold and calculating. "A tragic, unfortunate accident."

He began pacing the room, his mind racing, already formulating a plan. "We'll say she slipped and fell," he continued, his voice growing stronger. "Hit her head on the desk. It happens all the time."

I stared at him in disbelief. Was he serious? Did he really think we could cover up this crime? The blood on our hands, the chaos in the room, it all screamed of foul play.

But Robert was relentless, his desperation fueling his determination. "We have to protect ourselves," he said, his eyes pleading with me to understand. "We have to protect our family."

His words twisted in my gut, a sickening reminder of the lies and deceit that had defined his life. I had wanted to expose him, to bring him to justice. But now, I was being pulled into his web of deception, becoming an accomplice in his crime.

A wave of nausea washed over me. I wanted to scream, to run away, to pretend that none of this had ever happened. But I knew that I couldn't escape the consequences of my actions. I was trapped with no way out.

Robert's voice, though hushed, held a chilling determination that sent shivers down my spine. "We have no choice, Evelyn," he said, his eyes pleading with me to understand. "We have to protect ourselves. We have to protect our family."

I stared at him, my mind reeling. Could we really erase the evidence of our crime, rewrite the narrative of Katherine's death? A part of me, the part that still clung to a shred of morality, screamed in protest. But another part, the part that had been twisted and warped by my own thirst for revenge, whispered that perhaps this was the only way out.

Robert, sensing my hesitation, continued his persuasion. "Think of the children, Evelyn," he said, his voice softening. "They need us. They need a stable home, a loving family. If the truth comes out, their lives will be destroyed."

His words struck a chord within me. Olivia and Max, their innocent faces filled with trust and affection, flashed before my eyes. The thought of them being dragged into this nightmare, their lives forever scarred by the consequences of our actions, was unbearable.

I closed my eyes, taking a deep breath, trying to calm the turmoil within. When I opened them again, my resolve had hardened. I would do whatever it took to protect the children, even if it meant becoming an accomplice in Robert's crime.

"What do we need to do?" I asked, my voice barely a whisper.

A grim satisfaction flickered across Robert's face. He knew he had won me over. "First," he said, "we need to clean up this mess."

We worked in silence, the only sound the rhythmic swish of the mop as we scrubbed the bloodstains from the carpet. We righted the overturned furniture, carefully rearranging it to give the impression of a simple accident. We even managed to find a plausible explanation for the broken vase, claiming that Katherine had knocked it over in her fall.

As we worked, a sense of unreality washed over me. It was as if we were actors in a macabre play, following a script that had been written for us. But beneath the surface, a cold dread gnawed at me. Could we really pull this off? Could we deceive everyone, including the children?

When we were finished, the study looked almost normal, save for the lingering scent of bleach and the faintest hint of blood that clung to the air. Robert surveyed the room, a satisfied smirk playing on his lips. "Perfect," he said, clapping me on the shoulder. "No one will ever suspect a thing."

I forced a smile, but my heart was heavy with guilt and dread. We had covered up a crime, erased the evidence of our actions. But the truth, like a ghost, lingered in the shadows, waiting for its moment to emerge.

Robert, with his unnerving composure, had taken charge of the situation, orchestrating a macabre performance designed to shield us from the consequences of our actions. He instructed me to call for an ambulance, feigning panic and distress as I relayed a fabricated tale of a tragic accident.

I stumbled through the words, my voice thick with barely suppressed guilt and revulsion. The operator's calm reassurance, their promise of immediate assistance, only served to amplify the sickening knot in my stomach.

When the paramedics arrived, I watched as they examined Katherine's lifeless body, their faces etched with sympathy and concern. I had to turn away, unable to bear the weight of their innocent gazes. Robert, ever the composed actor, relayed the concocted story with chilling conviction, his voice trembling with feigned grief.

The children, roused from their slumber by the commotion, emerged from their rooms, their eyes wide with confusion and fear. I knelt beside Olivia, pulling her into a tight embrace, my own tears mingling with hers. "Mommy had an accident," I whispered, my voice choked with emotion. "She fell and hit her head."

Olivia's sobs intensified, her small body shaking with grief. Max, his face pale and drawn, clung to his sister, his eyes filled with a silent terror that mirrored my own.

As the paramedics loaded Katherine's body onto a stretcher, I watched as Robert comforted the children, his voice soothing and reassuring. It was a grotesque performance, a mockery of the love and devotion he had never truly shown her in life.

The house fell silent as the ambulance pulled away, leaving behind a gaping void that threatened to swallow us whole. The weight of our secret hung heavy in the air, suffocating us with its toxic fumes. I looked at Robert, his face etched with a mixture of grief and relief, and I knew that we were bound together by this shared burden, forever linked by the tragedy we had caused.

The children, oblivious to the truth, mourned their mother's untimely death, their innocent hearts shattered by the cruel hand of fate. But I knew the truth, the dark and twisted truth that lurked beneath the surface. And as I watched Robert comfort his children, a chilling realization dawned upon me: the real tragedy had only just begun.

In the aftermath of the staged accident, an oppressive silence settled over the Bennett household. The once vibrant home, filled with laughter and warmth, now felt like a mausoleum, haunted by the ghosts of our sins.

I moved through the motions of daily life like an automaton, my mind a relentless carousel of guilt and regret. The sight of Olivia and Max, their faces etched with sorrow, twisted a knife in my heart. They mourned their mother, their innocence shattered by a lie we had woven.

Robert, too, seemed to be crumbling under the weight of our shared secret. The confident facade he had always presented to the world had cracked, revealing a vulnerability I had never seen before. His eyes were haunted, his shoulders slumped with the burden of our deception.

We rarely spoke, our conversations limited to the bare necessities. The air between us crackled with unspoken accusations, our silence a deafening testament to the guilt that gnawed at our souls.

At night, I lay awake in my bed, tormented by nightmares of

Katherine's lifeless body, her blood staining my hands. I could hear Robert pacing in his room, his restless footsteps echoing through the empty house.

The weight of our secret was suffocating, a poisonous cloud that permeated every corner of our lives. It was a constant reminder of the darkness that lurked beneath the surface, a darkness we had created together.

I tried to find solace in the children, seeking refuge in their innocent embrace. But even their love couldn't erase the stain of guilt that clung to me. I saw the questions in their eyes, the unspoken yearning for answers that I couldn't provide.

Robert, on the other hand, seemed to retreat further into himself, seeking solace in work and alcohol. He became increasingly distant, his once warm demeanor replaced by a cold aloofness.

The cracks in our facades were widening, threatening to shatter the fragile illusion we had constructed. I knew that we couldn't continue like this, living a lie, haunted by the ghosts of our past. But the fear of exposure, of the consequences we would face if the truth were revealed, kept us trapped in this self-imposed prison.

The weight of our shared secret was a crushing burden, a cancer that was slowly eating away at our souls. We were both crumbling from the inside out, our lives unraveling with each passing day.

The days following Katherine's death were a blur of muted anguish and forced normalcy. The children, bless their innocent hearts, tried to find solace in routine, in the comforting familiarity of their home. Olivia, her eyes perpetually red-rimmed, sought refuge in her art, her canvases filling with dark, swirling strokes that mirrored the turmoil within her. Max, ever the stoic observer, retreated into a world of books, his young mind grappling with a grief he couldn't fully comprehend.

Their sorrow was a constant reminder of my own culpability. The guilt gnawed at me, a relentless parasite feeding on my soul. I watched them from the shadows, my heart aching with every tear they shed, every whispered question that went unanswered. I longed to comfort them, to tell them the truth, to beg for their forgiveness. But the fear of the consequences, of the pain it would cause them, held me back.

Robert, meanwhile, had become a tightly wound spring, his nerves frayed, his paranoia reaching fever pitch. He saw threats everywhere, his eyes darting suspiciously at every shadow, every creak of the floorboards. He barely slept, his nights filled with restless pacing and muttered whispers.

The once confident and charismatic businessman was now a shell of his former self, his energy consumed by the fear of exposure. He saw investigators in every stranger, conspiracy in every innocent remark. He became obsessed with maintaining the illusion of normalcy, his every action a carefully calculated performance designed to deflect suspicion.

The tension between us thickened with each passing day. The guilt that bound us together was also a source of unspoken resentment. I saw the accusation in his eyes, the blame he silently placed on me for the tragic turn of events. And though I shared his guilt, I also harbored a growing resentment towards him. It was his lies, his deceit, that had set this chain of events in motion.

The weight of our shared secret was a suffocating burden, a poison that seeped into every corner of our lives. It was a constant reminder of the darkness that lurked beneath the surface, a darkness that threatened to consume us both.

The cracks in our armor widened as the days turned into weeks, revealing the fragile and broken individuals beneath. We were both living a lie, trapped in a web of our own making.

CHAPTER 13

Justice and Redemption

E ach morning, I woke with a knot of dread in my stomach, a sense of impending doom hanging heavy in the air. The house now felt like a prison. The walls seemed to close in on me, suffocating me with the weight of my guilt. The children's innocent faces, etched with grief, haunted my every waking moment. Their trust, once so easily manipulated, now felt like a heavy burden I didn't deserve.

The more I observed Robert, the more I realized the depth of his depravity. His paranoia had escalated into a consuming obsession, his every action driven by a desperate need to preserve his facade. He had become a monster, his humanity buried beneath layers of deceit and self-preservation.

One evening, as I tucked Max into bed, he looked up at me with those trusting eyes, and I felt a pang of guilt so sharp it took my breath away. "Evelyn," he whispered, his voice trembling, "do you think Mommy is watching over us?"

I hesitated, my throat constricting with emotion. "I believe she is, Max," I managed to say, my voice barely a whisper.

He smiled, a sad, wistful smile that broke my heart. "I miss her so much," he said, his eyes filling with tears.

I pulled him close, my own tears streaming down my face. "I know you do, Max," I whispered, my voice choked with emotion. "I miss her too."

In that moment, I knew I couldn't continue down this path. I had become the very thing I despised, a liar, a manipulator, a destroyer of lives. The guilt had become an unbearable burden, a poison that was slowly killing me from the inside out.

I made a decision. I would confess. I would tell the authorities everything, no matter the consequences. I owed it to Katherine, to her children, and to myself. It was the only way to find redemption, to atone for my sins.

That night, under the cover of darkness, I crept into Robert's study. I found a blank sheet of paper and a pen, my hands shaking as I began to write. I poured out my heart, confessing every detail of my plan, every lie I had told, every manipulation I had employed. I didn't hold back, laying bare the depths of my guilt and remorse.

When I was finished, I sealed the letter in an envelope and addressed it to the police. I hesitated for a moment, the weight of my decision pressing down on me. But then, with a deep breath, I slipped the letter into my pocket, knowing that this was the first step towards redemption.

With the weight of the confession in my pocket, I moved through the darkened house like a phantom. The familiar rooms, once my stage for manipulation, now felt alien and oppressive. Every creak of the floorboards, every whisper of the wind through the eaves, seemed to echo the magnitude of my betrayal.

I crept into Olivia's room, the moonlight casting an ethereal glow on her sleeping form. I longed to wake her, to apologize for the pain I had caused, but I knew I couldn't. I had to leave, to vanish from their lives before the truth ripped them apart.

With a heavy heart, I placed a hand on her forehead, brushing a stray strand of hair from her face. "Forgive me," I whispered, my voice barely audible. "I never meant to hurt you."

I moved on to Max's room, my steps heavy with sorrow. He slept soundly, his arms wrapped around a worn teddy bear. A pang of guilt pierced my heart as I realized that I was abandoning him, leaving him to face the fallout of my actions.

I knelt beside his bed, my eyes welling up with tears. "Be strong, Max," I whispered, my voice choked with emotion. "Don't let the darkness consume you."

With a final, lingering glance at the children, I turned and left their rooms, my heart heavy with sorrow and regret. I moved through the house, gathering my few belongings, my movements swift and silent.

I paused in the doorway of Robert's study, the scene of our crime a chilling reminder of the darkness that had consumed us.

As I slipped out of the house, the first rays of dawn were beginning to break through the darkness. I walked away from the life I had built, the family I had grown to care for, and the man I had once sought to destroy.

I didn't look back, knowing that there was no turning back. I had made my choice, and now I had to face the consequences.

But as I walked away, I felt a glimmer of hope, a faint whisper of redemption. Perhaps, by confessing my sins, I could atone for the pain I had caused, and find a path towards healing and forgiveness.

The gravel crunched beneath my feet as I made my way down the long driveway, each step a farewell to the life I had crafted, the revenge I had so meticulously planned. The first rays of dawn painted the sky in hues of orange and pink, a stark contrast to the darkness that had consumed me for so long.

I reached the gate, my fingers tracing the cold metal bars. With one last look back at the imposing silhouette of the Bennett mansion, I slipped through the opening and into the anonymity of the world beyond.

I had no plan, no destination in mind. My only goal was to disappear, to vanish from the lives I had entangled myself in. I shed my uniform, the symbol of my deception, leaving it crumpled on the side of the road like a discarded snake skin.

I hailed a taxi, instructing the driver to take me to the nearest train station. As the city lights blurred past the window, I felt a strange sense of detachment, as if I were watching a movie of my own life.

I purchased a one-way ticket to a distant town, a place where no one knew my name or my past. I boarded the train, my heart heavy with a mixture of guilt, sorrow, and a flicker of hope.

As the train pulled away from the station, I watched the landscape rush by, the familiar landmarks fading into the distance. I was leaving behind a life built on lies, a revenge plot that had spiraled out of control. But I was also leaving behind the pain and the anger that had fueled my every action.

I didn't know what the future held, but I was determined to make amends for the harm I had caused. I would find a way to atone for my sins, to rebuild my life on a foundation of truth and integrity.

The train journey was long and arduous, a physical manifestation of the emotional turmoil that raged within me. I spent hours staring out the window, lost in a whirlwind of memories and regrets.

As the train finally pulled into the station, I stepped onto the platform, a stranger in a strange land. I had no money, no possessions, no identity. But I had something far more valuable – a chance to start over, to redeem myself, to find peace.

I took a deep breath, the crisp morning air filling my lungs. It was a new beginning, a chance to forge a new path, a path that led away from the darkness and towards the light. And as I walked away from the station, I knew that my journey towards redemption may have only just begun.

+ + +

The days following Evelyn's disappearance were a macabre dance of denial and dread. I clung to the hope that it was all a nightmare, that I would wake up and find Katherine by my side, her laughter filling the house with warmth. But reality was a cruel mistress, refusing to release me from the clutches of my guilt.

The investigation into Katherine's death was swift and relentless. The police, initially accepting the narrative of a tragic accident, soon began to ask questions, their suspicions piqued by inconsistencies in my account and the housekeeper's hushed whispers. I watched as the walls closed in, the net of suspicion tightening around me with each passing day.

The once thriving Bennett empire, built on a foundation of lies and deceit, began to crumble under the scrutiny of investigators and the relentless glare of the media. My business partners, sensing the impending collapse, distanced themselves, eager to protect their own interests.

The once grand mansion, a symbol of my success, now felt like a prison. The echoes of Katherine's laughter were replaced by the chilling silence of my own thoughts. I wandered through the empty rooms, haunted by the ghosts of my past, the victims of my ambition.

The children, their innocence shattered by their mother's death, withdrew into their own private worlds of grief and confusion. Olivia's paintings grew darker, her strokes filled with a raw anguish that mirrored my own. Max, his youthful exuberance replaced by a solemn silence, spent hours staring out the window, his gaze fixed on a horizon he could no longer see.

The night Evelyn's letter arrived, I knew it was the beginning of the end. As I read her confession, my hands trembled, my heart pounding in my chest. The truth, the ugly, damning truth, was laid bare before me.

I had been exposed, my carefully constructed facade shattered into a million pieces. The world I had built, the empire I had created, was collapsing around me. And I, the architect of my own destruction, was powerless to stop it.

As the police sirens wailed in the distance, I knew that my time was up. The consequences of my actions, the sins of my past, had finally caught up with me. I was facing arrest, ruin, the loss of everything I had ever worked for.

But more than anything, I was facing the truth. The truth of who I had become, the monster I had created in my relentless pursuit of power and wealth. And as the handcuffs clicked shut around my wrists, I knew that I had finally been brought to justice, not by Evelyn's revenge, but by my own actions. The housemaid was no longer the enemy; I was.

+++

The aftermath of my father's arrest felt like a relentless storm. The media swarmed our lives, stripping away any semblance of privacy we once had. Flashing cameras and probing microphones became our new reality. They camped outside our mansion, turning our home into a spectacle for the world to gawk at.

I withdrew into my art, my sanctuary in this chaos. My canvases transformed into vivid expressions of my anger and pain. Every stroke was a release, a cry for understanding in a world that suddenly felt so alien. My brother, Max, was a shadow of his former self, his innocence shattered. His silence was deafening, and his eyes, once so full of youthful curiosity, now held a depth of sorrow and wisdom far beyond his years.

The revelations of our father's crimes, the truth about our mother's death, hit us like a freight train. Our world, built on lies, crumbled, leaving us to pick up the pieces.

I felt a deep sense of betrayal. The man I had looked up to was a fraud. Worse, he was a murderer. My mother, my rock, had been his victim. The foundation of my life, my beliefs, was nothing but a facade hiding decay and deceit.

Yet, as the initial shock wore off, a steely resolve grew within me. I couldn't allow my father's sins to define me. I couldn't let the darkness of our past eclipse our future. With therapy, we began the painful journey of healing. We talked, we cried, we raged at the injustice. But we also found strength in our shared grief and determination.

My art evolved with me. The dark, tortured expressions on my canvas began to soften. Brighter colors, symbols of hope and resilience, started to emerge. It was my way of finding beauty in the pain, of turning my sorrow into something transformative.

Max, though still quiet and introspective, threw himself into his studies. His intellectual curiosity became a beacon of hope. His quiet strength was a source of inspiration for me.

The road to healing wasn't smooth. There were days when despair threatened to engulf us. But we clung to each other, our love and determination forming the bedrock of our new lives. The housemaid, whose actions had unraveled our family's secrets, was gone. But her revelations forced us to confront our reality, to face the truth about ourselves.

In the end, it was this confrontation that allowed us to heal, to rebuild. We emerged from the ashes of our tragedy stronger and more united than ever.

The world had shattered around me. First Mom, then Dad... everything I thought I knew was a lie. I locked myself away in my art studio, surrounded by half-finished canvases and the lingering scent of turpentine. The vibrant colors I once loved seemed dull and lifeless, a mockery of the emotions raging within me.

My escape had always been my art, a way to channel the pain and confusion that simmered beneath the surface. But now, even my art had betrayed me. My brushstrokes were erratic, my colors muddy, my vision clouded by a grief that refused to subside.

I sought solace in the bottle sometimes, the familiar burn of alcohol a temporary reprieve from the agonizing reality of my life. I drank to forget, to numb the pain, to silence the voices in my head that whispered of betrayal and loss. But the escape was fleeting, the hangover a cruel reminder of my weakness. Each morning, I woke with a pounding headache and a soul weighed down by guilt and despair. I looked at myself in the mirror, disgusted by the hollow-eyed stranger staring back at me.

One day, as I stumbled through the wreckage of my studio, my eyes fell upon a half-finished portrait of my mother. It was a beautiful piece, capturing her gentle smile and loving eyes. A wave of grief washed over me, and I sank to the floor, sobbing uncontrollably.

In that moment of raw vulnerability, I saw a glimmer of hope. I realized that I couldn't continue down this destructive path. I couldn't let my mother's memory be tarnished by my own self-destruction. I reached out to my brother, Max, the one person who truly understood the depth of my pain. He held me as I cried, his silent strength a comforting presence in the midst of chaos.

With Max's support, I took the first tentative steps towards recovery. I sought professional help, attending therapy sessions and support groups. It wasn't easy. The road to recovery was long and arduous, filled with setbacks and moments of despair. But I was determined to overcome my addiction, to honor my mother's memory by reclaiming my life.

With each passing day, I felt a glimmer of hope returning. The fog of addiction began to lift, revealing a newfound clarity and strength. I started painting again, my brushstrokes bolder, my colors brighter, my vision infused with a newfound hope.

I knew that I would never forget the pain of my past, the trauma of losing my parents. But I also knew that I could choose to rise above it, to transform my pain into something beautiful and meaningful.

While I found my escape in art and the haze of addiction, Max sought refuge in the quiet corners of the house, his nose buried in books far beyond his years. He was always an old soul, my little brother, observing the world with a quiet intensity that often unnerved me. But now, in the wake of our shared tragedy, his maturity bloomed, his strength becoming a lifeline in the turbulent sea of our grief.

I'd often find myself curled up in my studio, surrounded by a chaotic mess of paint and canvases, my eyes vacant and unseeing. Without a word, Max would sit beside me, his small hand finding mine, a silent offering of comfort. He'd read to me from his books, his voice a steady rhythm in the deafening silence of my despair. His words, though often beyond my comprehension, seemed to weave a tapestry of hope and resilience, a lifeline to a world I had all but abandoned.

Max became my anchor, his quiet strength a stark contrast to my emotional turmoil. He cooked simple meals, his small hands meticulously following recipes he found in our mother's worn cookbook. He cleaned the house, his methodical movements a soothing balm to my chaotic mind. He even took over the task of caring for our neglected garden, coaxing life back into the withered plants with a tenderness that belied his age.

It was as if he had become the adult, the caretaker, the one responsible for holding our fractured family together. And as I watched him, a flicker of admiration ignited within me, a spark of hope that maybe, just maybe, we could survive this ordeal.

One evening, as we sat together in the dimly lit living room, Max looked up from his book, his eyes filled with a wisdom that belied his years. "Olivia," he said, his voice soft yet firm, "we can't let this destroy us. We have to be strong for each other."

His words pierced through the fog of my despair, a beacon of light in the darkness. He was right. We couldn't let our parents' mistakes define us. We had to find a way to move forward, to create a new life out of the ashes of the old.

Max, with his quiet wisdom and unwavering support, had become my rock, my guiding light. Together, we navigated the treacherous waters of grief and loss, our bond strengthening with each passing day.

The echoes of our shattered past lingered in the hallowed halls of the Bennett mansion, a constant reminder of the love we had lost and the betrayal we had endured. But amidst the pain and the grief, a new kind of resilience began to take root. We, the children of this fractured family, found solace and strength in each other's company.

The house, once a symbol of opulence and deceit, gradually transformed into a haven of healing. We cleared out the clutter of our parents' lives, discarding the material possessions that had once held so much importance. We repainted the walls in warm, soothing colors, filling the rooms with light and life.

We established new traditions and simple rituals that bound us together and created a sense of normalcy in a world that had been turned upside down. We cooked meals together, our laughter filling the once-silent kitchen. We played board games in the living room, our competitive spirit a welcome distraction from the weight of our grief. We shared stories and memories, our voices weaving a tapestry of love and resilience.

The garden, once neglected and overgrown, became a symbol of our rebirth. Max, with his newfound passion for horticulture, spent hours tending to the plants, his green thumb coaxing life back into the barren soil. We planted a rose bush in memory of our mother, its delicate blooms are a testament to her enduring love.

With each passing day, the pain of our loss began to lessen, the wounds of betrayal slowly healing. We found strength in our shared grief, our bond deepening with every tear we shed, every memory we shared.

We were not the same family we had once been. The scars of our past would forever remain, a reminder of the darkness we had endured. But we were survivors, forged in the crucible of adversity. We had learned the true meaning of family, and the importance of love, trust, and forgiveness.

We were the Bennett children, forever changed, but not broken. We had weathered the storm, and we had emerged stronger and more resilient than ever before. We were ready to face the future, to forge a new path, a path built on the foundations of love, hope, and unwavering support for each other.

EPILOGUE

One Year Later

The steel bars cast long shadows across the cold, sterile floor of my cell. A year had passed since my world imploded since the truth of my sins had been laid bare. I, Robert Bennett, once a titan of industry, a man of power and influence, was now nothing more than a number, a prisoner confined to a cage of my own making.

The silence of my cell was a stark contrast to the hustle and bustle of the life I had once led. Gone were the boardroom meetings, the lavish parties, the constant hum of activity that had surrounded me. In their place was a deafening quietude, broken only by the occasional clang of metal doors and the muffled voices of other inmates.

In this isolation, I had ample time to reflect on the choices I had made and the path I had taken. The memories of my past life haunted me, a constant reminder of the man I had been, the man I had become.

I thought of Katherine, her gentle smile, her unwavering love for our children. The guilt gnawed at me, a constant ache in my soul. I had betrayed her trust, and destroyed her life, all in the name of greed and ambition.

I thought of Olivia and Max, their innocent faces etched with the pain of loss and betrayal. I had failed them as a father, my actions casting a long shadow over their lives. The knowledge that I had caused them so much pain was a heavy burden to bear.

But even in the depths of my despair, I found a glimmer of

hope. I had received letters from the children, their words filled with love and forgiveness. They told me of their struggles, their triumphs, their determination to build a new life out of the ashes of the old.

Olivia had blossomed into a talented artist, her paintings a testament to her resilience and strength. Max, ever the scholar, had excelled in his studies, his intellect a beacon of hope in a world filled with darkness.

They had found a way to heal, to forgive, to move forward. And in their resilience, I found a glimmer of redemption for myself.

I had been a monster, a man consumed by greed and ambition. But I was also a father, a husband, a human being capable of love and remorse. And in the quiet solitude of my cell, I made a vow to change, to become a better man, to make amends for the harm I had caused.

I knew that the road to redemption would be long and arduous. But I was determined to take the first step, to acknowledge my sins, to seek forgiveness, and to make the most of the time I had left.

The bars of my cell may confine my body, but they cannot imprison my spirit. I may be a prisoner, but I am also a father, a man who still can love and hope. And in that hope, I find a glimmer of light in the darkness of my past.

The steel bars felt cold against my cheek as I pressed them against them, seeking a fleeting connection to the outside world. The prison walls were a constant reminder of my isolation, of the chasm that separated me from the life I had once known.

Each day, I woke to the same monotonous routine. The clang of metal doors, the shuffling of footsteps, and the sterile smell of disinfectant permeated every corner of this concrete tomb. I ate my meals in silence, the bland food a stark contrast to the lavish feasts I had once enjoyed.

But it wasn't the physical confinement that tormented me the most. It was the memories, the ghosts of my past that haunted me relentlessly. I saw Katherine's face in every shadow and heard her laughter in the whispers of the wind. The guilt was a constant companion, a gnawing ache that refused to subside.

I had built my life on a foundation of lies and deceit, sacrificing love and integrity for power and wealth. I had betrayed the woman I loved, the mother of my children, driven by a blind ambition that had consumed my soul.

In the quiet solitude of my cell, I was forced to confront the darkness that had festered within me for so long. The man I saw reflected in the steel mirror was a stranger, a hollow shell of the person I once thought I was.

The nights were the worst. Sleep eluded me, replaced by a relentless replay of my mistakes, and my regrets. I saw Katherine's lifeless body, her blood staining my hands. I heard Olivia's sobs, and Max's heartbroken whispers.

I had destroyed everything I held dear, and for what? A fleeting taste of power, a hollow victory that had turned to ashes in my mouth.

In the depths of my despair, I found solace in the letters from my children. They were brief, carefully worded missives, but they offered a glimmer of hope in the darkness. Olivia wrote of her art, her paintings a testament to her resilience and strength. Max shared his academic achievements, and his thirst for knowledge a beacon of light in a world filled with shadows.

Their words were a reminder of the love that still existed, the bond that even my betrayal could not sever. They had found a way to forgive, to heal, to move forward. And in their strength, I found a flicker of hope for my redemption.

I knew that I could never undo the harm I had caused, never

erase the pain I had inflicted. But I could strive to be a better man, a man worthy of the love and forgiveness that had been so generously offered. I could use my time in prison to reflect, to learn, to grow.

Perhaps, one day, I would be able to atone for my sins, to make amends for the damage I had caused. Perhaps, one day, I would be able to look at my children with pride, knowing that I had finally become the father they deserved. But for now, all I could do was endure the silence of my cell, haunted by the choices I had made.

+++

The revelation of Evelyn's letter was a shockwave that reverberated through the fractured remnants of our family. It laid bare the truth of our mother's death, exposing the dark underbelly of deceit that had poisoned our lives.

The initial wave of anger and betrayal was followed by a profound sense of sadness and loss. We mourned for our mother, for the life she had been robbed of, for the love and care she would never be able to give. We mourned for the innocence we had lost, for the shattered illusions of a perfect family.

But amid our grief, there was also a sense of closure. Evelyn's confession, though painful, provided the missing pieces of the puzzle, the answers to the questions that had haunted us for so long. We finally knew the truth, the whole truth, and in that knowledge, we found a strange sense of peace.

We never heard from Evelyn again. She vanished from our lives as suddenly as she had appeared, leaving behind only the echo of her confession and the lingering scent of her betrayal. But despite the pain she had caused, I couldn't bring myself to hate her.

In a way, I understood her motives, her thirst for revenge. I had seen the darkness that lurked beneath my father's polished facade, the cruelty he was capable of. I knew that he had wronged her mother, and had caused her unimaginable pain.

But Evelyn's actions, though understandable, were not justifiable. She had taken an innocent life, shattered our family, and left us to pick up the pieces. Yet, I couldn't deny the strange sense of gratitude I felt towards her. Her confession freed us from the shackles of doubt and uncertainty, allowing us to grieve openly and honestly.

In the end, Evelyn's disappearance was a fitting conclusion to her story. She was a ghost from the past, a specter of vengeance that had haunted our lives for far too long. Her absence allowed us to move on, to heal, to rebuild our lives on a foundation of truth and authenticity.

We will never forget her, nor the pain she had caused. But we would also remember her as the catalyst for our liberation, the woman who, through her betrayal, had inadvertently set us free.

As we picked up the pieces of our lives, the question of Evelyn's fate lingered in the air, an unspoken mystery that hung heavy in our hearts.

We never heard from her again, no word, no sign, no trace of her existence. She vanished into thin air, leaving behind a void that couldn't be filled.

In the quiet moments, I found myself wondering about her, imagining her wandering the streets, a ghost of her former self. Had she found the peace she sought? Had she managed to escape the demons of her past?

Or was she still haunted by the events that had unfolded in our home, the weight of her actions a constant burden? Was she running, forever looking over her shoulder, afraid of the consequences that might catch up to her?

I tried to imagine her finding solace in a new life, far away from the pain and betrayal that had defined her existence. Perhaps she had found a place where she could start anew, where she could shed the weight of her past and forge a new identity.

Or perhaps, she had been consumed by the darkness, her guilt and remorse a never-ending torment. Maybe she was lost, wandering, searching for a redemption that seemed forever out of reach.

The uncertainty of her fate was a constant reminder of the fragility of life, and the unpredictability of the human heart. It was a reminder that even in the darkest of times, there is always the possibility of redemption, of finding a path toward healing and forgiveness.

But it was also a reminder of the consequences of our actions, the ripple effects that can reverberate through the lives of others. Evelyn's choices had irrevocably changed our lives, leaving a scar that would never fully heal.

And so, the question of her fate remained unanswered, a lingering mystery that would forever haunt the halls of the Bennett mansion. But even in the absence of answers, there was a sense of closure, a quiet acceptance of the unknown.

We had learned to live with the scars of our past and to embrace the uncertainty of the future. We had found strength in our resilience, in our ability to adapt and overcome. And in that strength, we found a glimmer of hope, a belief that even in the darkest of times, there is always the possibility of light.

A LETTER FROM VICTORIA

Dearest readers,

Wow! I'm so thrilled you chose to read *The Housemaid Is the Enemy*. Thank you from the bottom of my heart.

If you want to stay in the loop about my upcoming Peartree releases and special deals, please sign up and follow my author page

I truly hope you loved reading *The Housemaid Is the Enemy*. If you did, would you consider leaving a review? Your thoughts mean the world to me, and they help new readers discover my stories.

And, of course, you can follow me on Amazon to see all my books and to get the scoop on any price drops.

With so much gratitude,

Victoria

ACKNOWLEDGMENTS

I can hardly believe that I have finally finished this book. It wasn't an easy journey, but it was worth every moment.

First and foremost, I want to thank the team at Peartree for your tireless work in bringing *The Housemaid Is the Enemy* to life. A special thanks to Mary Toon for her incredible insights into my writing. Your feedback has been invaluable.

A big thank you to my literary agent, Josh Clan, and my colleagues who always believed in me and supported me. Your encouragement means the world to me.

Thank you to all the people who reviewed the manuscript during the editing process: my mother, Kate, Emy, and Ben. I'm sure you probably got tired of me always handing you my script to review. So, I just want you to know how grateful I am for your patience and feedback.

Finally, a million thanks to my incredibly supportive readers! This is all because of you.

We – both author and publisher – hope you enjoyed this book. We believe that you can become a reader at any time in your life, and we'd love your help to give the next generation a head start.

Published by Peartree in 2024

Made in the USA
Columbia, SC
14 August 2024

4ee4559b-c697-431c-9828-fb48fd4b6ef6R01